SOUVIENS

BARBARA DARLING SAXENA

ISBN-10: 1492138126
ISBN 13: 9781492138129

*This novel is dedicated to the
memory of the thirty-four souls who
perished in the 1934 Hotel Kerns Fire,
and to the seventy-two firemen
who risked their lives battling the inferno.*

With Love and Gratitude to:

My father, Ernest, my hero and a wonderful storyteller,

My husband, Yogi, my best friend,

My daughter, Margot, my greatest gift,

Our Golden Dogs, my constant sunshine

ONE

Lansing, Michigan
Friday, August 6, 2010
7:05 PM

D akota awoke with the familiar adrenalin rush from another one of her "movies". Ever since she was eight years old when she had lost her family in a motor vehicle accident, she had been plagued by recurring nightmares. She had been paraded in front of numerous counselors, teachers, and other well meaning adults, but to no avail. During one such session, it had been suggested that she view these nightmares as "movies" for her enjoyment. As she wiped off the sweat beads from her forehead, and untangled the blankets from her legs, she could not imagine making such a silly suggestion to one of her patients. The nightmares felt more like a reality show from hell, where she could experience it with all of her five senses.

Luckily for this busy thirty-three year old doctor, "Dak" Graham, as her patients affectionately called her, the dreams had become less frequent as she grew older. In fact, this was the first episode in several weeks. She willed herself to move out of the haze and headed to the bathroom to get ready for her date that night. Dakota had hoped a quick nap after her long work day would rejuvenate her; but instead, she felt drained and tempted to cancel out. But Dakota could think of no excuse to make, and she did not want to share her nightmares with others.

Her date for the evening was her new friend of six weeks, Alex Zahn. They had met at "Scrap Fest" during the Festival of the Moon held in Lansing's Old Town. Contestants were given a week to collect scrap metal from a scrap yard, and two weeks to turn their materials into large works of art. She was critiquing the various pieces with her cousin Morgan when Alex jumped in on the conversation. Before Dakota knew it, Morgan had conveniently excused herself to go home to her twin boys and husband. Dakota found herself browsing through Old Town's art shops and dining under the moon while getting to know Alex better.

Ever since, Dakota and Alex had touched base almost daily by phone, and saw each other most Friday nights. Despite Alex's encouragement, Dakota had kept things fairly platonic. She was still stinging from a recent four year relationship breakup. However, she had to admit that Alex had brought some sparkle into her otherwise workaholic lifestyle.

Thirty minutes later, she was exiting her condominium. Her black, shoulder length bob haircut swung freely as she hurried out onto Michigan Avenue. She had inherited the family's short, slender genes, as her cousin Morgan would say, who towered over Dakota at nearly six feet tall.

Dakota could hear the national anthem being sung at Lansing's Lugnut Stadium which stood directly across from her condo. She had chosen her unit due to the balcony facing the ball park, and enjoyed sitting in the summer night, listening to the sounds of America's game. She quickly moved west along Michigan Avenue, and made a left onto Washington Avenue, hoping that Alex had not been waiting too long.

She pushed open the heavy wooden door decorated with a Celtic cross to enter Kelly's Irish Pub. She spotted Alex, standing at the far end of the mahogany bar that occupied the middle of the room. Alex was, as Morgan called him, a hunk. In his thirty's, he was tall and muscular, with his brown wavy hair perpetually messy looking. But it was his brilliant blue eyes that really attracted attention.

Alex was currently huddled against an Angelina Jolie look alike. Alex and the woman looked intent and very comfortable with each other; and Dakota felt a momentary twinge of jealously. But she reminded herself that Alex was perfectly free to see others. Alex caught Dakota's gaze, and stood up to motion her over. As Dakota approached, Alex reached over to grab her hand and drew her towards the bar.

"Dakota, I'd like you to meet Erin's mother, Cynthia, "said Alex.

"Nice to meet you, Cynthia. You have a wonderful daughter." Dakota extended her hand to Alex's ex-wife which was left hanging in mid air.

Cynthia slid behind Alex, kissed his cheek, and said "Alex, I'll bring Erin by tomorrow around noon. Enjoy your evening, Darling."

As Cynthia melted away into the crowd, Alex smiled a little uncomfortably. "I'm sorry if that was awkward for you. We had a few issues to discuss, and I thought we'd be done before you arrived...She can be a little standoffish at times..."

"Don't worry about it. "

They found themselves an empty booth, ordered some drinks and two cherry burgers. In between bites of pub fries, Alex said, "Cynthia and I have a complicated relationship".

Alex was obviously still dwelling on his ex-wife, thought Dakota. Dakota had enjoyed an outing with his ten year old daughter, but had never heard Alex talk about his ex-wife before. "How so?"

"We had a business together when we were married. I was an architect, with a builder's license. I specialized in renovating old buildings, with architectural significance."

Dakota's interest was piqued. She had only known him as a talented artisan with a successful shop in Old Town. "What happened to your business?"

"That's the complicated part. I handled the technical aspects of the business, recruiting crews, approving design plans, and finding clients. I left the financial aspect in her hands. She was a paralegal with business experience, and I thought she could handle things. That's where I made my mistake."

He took a swig of his beer and seemed to be lost in his thoughts. Dakota remained quiet until he began speaking again. "We decided to up the ante from working on area houses and small offices, to larger buildings and landmarks. We started taking on contracts statewide, not just in Lansing. This required more upfront cash, before any profits would be seen. So we did the American thing and mortgaged our souls.

To make a long story short, we over leveraged our business and couldn't pay bills on time. "

"That must have been so hard to let your dream go."

"That was the least of it. Cynthia never told me the financial shape we were in. Whether it was pride or her wanting to be in control, she hid the mess from me. She kited checks and used money from one project to pay bills on other projects. Well, before long, the whole mess collapsed. I managed to repair some of the damage, but there were enough complaints about me that my license was suspended for two years."

"Cynthia is the one who made the bad decisions, and you were the one who was punished."

"She is Erin's mother, someone I used to love...Protecting her came naturally."

Dakota took Alex's hand and they sat silently for awhile, mulling over their conversation. "Do you mind if we make it an early evening tonight? It has been a long day," Alex asked.

Dakota agreed, and after paying their bill, they strolled back to her condominium.

"Sorry I've been a party pooper tonight," he said.

"I'm pretty tired too. Would you like to have some of Morgan's homemade cinnamon rolls before heading home?"

"Only if I can have them for breakfast," he said with a slight grin.

"I'm just not ready to get into another relationship yet. I can understand if you don't want to hang out anymore together," she offered.

"You're not getting rid of me that easily, Dakota. You're a fascinating and beautiful woman, definitely worth the wait." And with that, he blew her a kiss and left.

Dakota walked to her mailbox in the lobby and collected several days' worth of mail. She certainly was behind on all of life's tasks. Once inside her home, she kicked off her heels and plopped into her oversized loveseat. She clicked on the television and idly shuffled through her mail. She saw several bills that needed paying, amid lots of junk mail and magazines. About to toss the pile onto the end table for another day, something caught her eye. It was an envelope with formally embossed stationary. The return address was marked as Henderson, Russell and

Powell, Attorneys at Law, Boji Tower, 124 West Allegan Street, Lansing, Michigan.

Dakota suddenly felt chilled despite the warm summer night. She knew of no patients filing a malpractice case against her, but her hands shook nonetheless as she opened the envelope.

"Dear Dr. Graham," the letter read, "You are requested to attend the Reading of the Will for the Estate of Fenton S. Anderson, the thirty-first of August, 2010, at 3:00 PM. "

What was this...some kind of practical joke, she wondered? Only televison shows and movies had actual reading of wills. And who was this Fenton S. Anderson anyway? Dakota felt agitated, but she could not explain why. She stood up and began pacing around the living room, her heart pounding and her respirations rapid. And then, the sensations began in full force. Her first nightmare occurred while she was wide awake.

TWO

"Fenton Anderson, you get out of that tree this instant!" his mother Augusta demanded, , with a tone that left no question of the consequences of disobeying. Eleven year old Fenton had climbed up to his tree house in his Sunday best, no doubt to impress their guest, Grace. It was obvious that Fenton was smitten with Grace, five years his senior.

"Hurry on in, and eat your breakfast. We leave for Church soon."

"Yes, Mother," Fenton grumbled under his breath, clearly embarrassed by the reprimand.

Nothing would have made Augusta happier than to see these two married some day. Grace was the only child of her dear childhood friend, Clara. Clara and Augusta had been inseparable as youths, but their lives had taken very different paths. Augusta had married Sanford Anderson, a solid man, an heir to a lumber fortune that guaranteed a life without want. Clara, on the other hand, had married for love to Adam Dunning, a dreamer whose ideas never quite panned out. Yet despite their financial struggles, Clara had seemed very happy until she succumbed to the 1918 Spanish Flu epidemic.

Since Clara's death, Augusta had included Grace in many of their family activities. Adam had abandoned his fanciful pursuits, and had obtained a steady job at the Reo Motor Car Company.. He had even worked himself into a foreman position. The one promise Adam had made to Clara on her death bed was that Grace would go to college, and Adam was determined to see this promise through. He would frequently pick up extra shifts at Reo in order to add to the college savings account.

"Grace, come walk with me,, and tell me about your studies at school."

"Mrs. Anderson, did you know that scientists are working on a vaccine to protect people against whooping cough? Before long, I'm confident that there will be a vaccine that would have protected my mother from influenza. I hope to attend The University of Michigan Medical School and work on vaccine research," Grace proclaimed.

Oh my, such a serious girl, thought Augusta.

As the two of them walked arm and arm up to the house, the telephone was ringing inside. Sanford answered, his brow soon becoming deeply furrowed. He slowly replaced the receiver. He stared ahead, and wondered how he was ever going to tell Grace that her father had just died in an accident that morning.

THREE

As she drove the sixty mile trip from Lansing to Grand Rapids, Dakota mentally reviewed her web search results on Fenton S. Anderson. Born ninety-five years ago with the proverbial silver spoon in his mouth, the handsome and smooth talking young man had been know as the Heartthrob of the Midwest. A confirmed bachelor for many years, there were numerous photos of him with the glamour girls of Hollywood.

But to his credit, he had not simply squandered his father's fortune. He had parlayed the lumber business money into successful auto supply companies to feed Michigan's booming auto industry. In later years, he had shrewdly begun buying small startup companies specializing in alternative energy and electric car battery technologies.

She pulled into a parallel parking slot in the Heritage Hill section of downtown Grand Rapids, and fished her large purse for quarters for the meter. She studied the lovely Queen Anne style home, converted to the office of psychiatrist Dr. Peter Cho. Since her last visit here nearly two years ago, she was pleased to see the beaded spindles and lacy ornamental details were freshly painted. She thought how Alex would love exploring this area, one of the largest historical districts in the United States.

Thinking of Alex caused a stab of guilt. When he had asked her to join him for lunch today, she had lied that she was tied up with a house call. Not even her closest confident Morgan knew about her treks to Grand Rapids over the years to see Dr. Cho.

Dakota entered into the parlor area of the home that was now used as a waiting room. Before she could sit down, Dr. Cho came trotting down the hall way. "Eliza, it is so good to see you. Please come on in."

There was a barely discernible pause before Dakota turned around and reached out to shake his hand. She had forgotten that she had used her mother's name to assure her anonymity. He led her back to his private office, the original library of the house. The rows of mahogany book cases were somehow soothing while discussing uncomfortable topics.

As they settled into comfortable overstuffed leather chairs, he said, "It's been a long time... How have you been?"

"Fine..." She looked at the floor for a bit in silence, her eyes misting over. "Well, I was doing better...The nightmares were spacing out...And we had exhausted every conceivable test, from a brain MRI, and PET scan, to an EEG, sleep study, hypnosis, and blood tests...I was feeling like a lab experiment. And quite frankly, I was going broke. My friends would save for a cruise, while I was struggling to pay for medical bills. I just decided these nightmares were something I would have to learn to live with..."

"And then what happened?" Dr. Cho coaxed.

"I know you see lots of patient, so I don't expect you to remember my whole story. My nightmares began soon after my parents and brother died. They were so vivid, not like a normal dream that is hazy and lacking detail. I don't just see a building burning, but I can feel the waves of heat on my skin... I can smell the burning wood and flesh... I can taste soot on my lips... I can hear the screams. The screams are the worst part. And when I wake up, the memory doesn't fade as the day goes on, like a normal dream is soon forgotten. "

"Eliza, it's very kind of you to help this old man's memory. But I remember the details of your case quite well. In fact, I have been thinking a lot about you recently. But before I go on, I suspect there is something new that prompted your return visit today."

"Yes, that's true. Life was going pretty well. I love my work and spending time with my family. My boyfriend had decided we weren't a good fit anymore, but in hindsight, that was a good move for me as well. I was even starting to make new friends...And then, I received this letter in the mail that seemed to turn everything upside down again."

"I don't understand," Dr. Cho said.

"Before, the nightmares occurred while I was asleep. I would be alone, unobserved, so I could deal with them on my own. But now, I am getting the dreams while wide awake!" And with that, Dakota's pent up frustrations came crashing out in sobs.

Dr. Cho kindly handed her a box of tissues and sat quietly as Dakota's shoulders shook. She was so tired of carrying this burden alone.

After several minutes, she was able to speak again. "There was a time I could hear screaming when I was at work. I smelled weird odors while grocery shopping. How am I supposed to keep this secret when it is invading my waking hours?"

"During our last session, we had talked about the increased stress of hiding these nightmares from those you love. Did you ever share your problem with your boyfriend or cousin? "Dr. Cho asked.

"No...I suspect this was actually a factor in my breakup. I never wanted to sleep with my boyfriend because of the fear of a nightmare happening. I would always make up some excuse why I needed to leave, or why he couldn't stay...He told me during an argument that he had never heard of a girl who didn't like to cuddle after sex."

"Eliza-"

"Dakota," she injected.

"Excuse me?"

"My name is really Dakota. I used my mother's first name and drove here from Lansing, all due to my fear of others knowing my secret."

"And can I guess your occupation? I have suspected for a long time that you are a fellow physician...by the way you speak, by your reluctance to ever try medications to stop the nightmares, and your worry that others will realize you are not perfect, in other words, human," he said with a slight smile.

"Touché, Dr. Cho". She could feel her shoulders relaxing. The truth was always the best antidote.

"I am curious why you think a letter was the trigger for your new symptoms," said Dr. Cho.

"I was sent an invitation for the reading of the will for the estate of Fenton S. Anderson."

Dr. Cho let out a low whistle. "You have some powerful and influential friends. I read about his recent death in the Detroit Free Press."

"I had never heard of Fenton Anderson before, so I started researching him on line. I couldn't find any personal ties to members of his family either. He married at forty-nine years old to a Detroit car show model more than half his age named Candace Rogers. He has a son named Joel, forty-one years old, divorced, without kids. I can't play the six degree of separation game with me and this cast of characters."

"Have you asked any of your family about possible connections?"

"I was raised by my mother's parents. Grandpa Jacob has passed away, and Grandma Charlotte is in a nursing home with Alzheimer's. But Grandma Charlotte's younger sister, Aunt Charity, is doing well. She may be a good source of information."

Dr. Cho sat in silent thought for a moment. "Getting back to the letter, how did this unusual invitation play into the matter at hand?"

"Minutes after opening the letter, I started sensing the fire while awake for the first time...And the name Fenton provokes really strong emotions that I just can't explain. Nutty, I know."

Dr. Cho stood up and gazed out the window. "Over the years, I have tried without success to diagnose and treat your condition. At first glance, I thought it was night terrors. But it didn't fit the pattern. Those patients wake up terrified, but generally can't remember the details of the dream. We ruled out brain tumors, epilepsy, schizophrenia, and a host of other disorders..."

He walked towards his desk, pulled out a three ring binder, and returned to his chair. "Several months ago, I attended a conference about memory issues. It had the usual speakers that discussed the various forms of dementia. But there was a break out session with somewhat of an unorthodox scientist who had some pretty wild ideas on the origins of memories....Some of what he discussed reminded me of your nightmares. Could these images you see actually be memories coming out in the form of dreams?"

Dakota sat perplexed. How could these images be memories? She had never seen any burning buildings, and avoided any type of flame as much as possible.

Dr. Cho opened the binder and pulled out a business card tucked inside the cover. "The speaker's name is Dr. Theo Everett. He is a MD, with a PhD in neurobiology. Without divulging any private information, I briefly described a patient I had that has vivid dreams she can't explain. He became almost giddy when I asked if he would ever meet with us as a consultation. Of course, when I tried to contact you with the demographics you supplied here, I ran into a dead end. But Dr. Everett continues to call me on a regular basis to see if you have agreed to a meeting."

On one hand, Dakota felt terrified of inviting a stranger into their confidence to discuss her secrets. On the other hand, she felt a glimmer of hope that someone could help shed light on her problem.

Sensing her hesitation, Dr. Cho said, "Think about it for awhile... But in the mean time, tell me more about Fenton Anderson."

FOUR

"By the way, Fenton stopped by while you were out today," said Louise Mann, as she cleared the dinner plates to the sink. "He wanted to wish you a happy New Year."

Twenty four year old Grace Dunning began dipping the plates in the soapy suds. Even though she was one of the boarders in the Charles Mann home, she felt more like a family member and usually helped with the clean up.

"He is so handsome," gushed Louise. "And so charming...I've never understood your reluctance to encourage his interest in you."

Since her father's death eight years ago, Grace had lived at the Mann's Boarding House. The profits from selling their family home had allowed Grace to complete her bachelor's degree in Applied Science at Michigan State College and to afford her living expenses. But as close as Grace felt to Louise, it was conversations like this one that made Grace feel alone in the world.

Grace replied, "Fenton is a sweet young man, and I care about him very much. But I think of him more as a younger brother. Besides, we don't have common interests. And it aggravates me to no end how he is wasting his college education. He is more interested in the silly shenanigans of his fraternity than his class work. "

"Oh Grace, sometimes I can't believe you are six years younger than me! You should be having some fun in your life. There is plenty of time ahead for drudgery." And with that, Louise splashed some soapy water onto Grace. The women giggled, and then finished cleaning up in silence.

When the last dish was put away, Grace picked up the Lansing State Journal and walked into the front parlor. She and the Manns often enjoyed going out to the movies for an afternoon show. As she was looking for the theatre information, a headline grabbed her attention. The article discussed the Zonta Club of Lansing which "will assist women and girls who are looking forward to professional, business careers". The article also stated that "many talks on vocational guidance have been given during past year".

Grace felt a surge of excitement. She had never given up on her dream of attending medical school at The University of Michigan, despite the obstacles thrown in her way and the lack of support from others. With the help of a good recommendation from Sanford Anderson, she was currently working as a bank teller at the new Bank of Lansing. She needed to replenish her college fund before applying to medical school. But perhaps members of the Zonta Club would have some other helpful suggestions. If nothing else, it would be so refreshing to talk to others understanding of her dream.

Louise walked into the parlor to find Grace intently studying the newspaper. Grace had recently splurged on a new stylish Croquignole perm for one dollar. Her dark hair was cut very short, with ringlets high on her neck and sides. Louise thought Grace was pretty enough to be a movie star, yet Grace seemed oblivious to her beauty.

"So what's playing at the theatres today?" asked Louise.

Grace shuffled the papers around a little. "Let's see...playing at the Strand Theatre is 'Going Hollywood' with Bing Crosby and Marion Davies."

"How about...if we double date... with you and Fenton...and me and Charles", Louise drawled.

Grace rolled her eyes and tossed a sofa pillow at Louise.

FIVE

Lansing, Michigan
Tuesday, August 31, 2010
2:30 pm

Dakota sat nibbling her oatmeal cookie in Biggby's Coffee Shop, gazing out the window at the Boji Towers. Her meeting at the law office was in thirty minutes.

"Morgan, I can't believe you rappelled down that twenty-three story building in June," commented Dakota. Morgan had been part of a charity fundraiser where eighty people climbed down Lansing's tallest building.

At thirty-six years old, her cousin Morgan was the picture of health. She still wore her long blonde hair pulled back in a high pony tail, just as she did when playing center for Michigan State University's women's basketball team. "The twins thought I looked like Spider Man," said Morgan.

"Thanks for meeting me for lunch. Did you get a chance to ask your Mom if she had ever heard of Fenton Anderson?" asked Dakota, as they cleared their table.

"Mom's still up North at Mackinac Island for the week, but I promise to be Nancy Drew as soon as she comes home."

The two women left the coffee shop and hugged on the street, with Dakota promising to call with a good story later that night. Dakota crossed Allegan Street and entered the arched entrance of the brick and lime stone building. Completed in 1931, the Boji Towers, formerly known as the Olds Tower, was a good example of the Art Deco style sky scrapers of the era.

She entered the elevator that would take her to the law offices of Henderson, Russell, and Powell. Once the elevator door opened, she saw that the law offices occupied the entire floor. She walked over to the reception desk and identified herself.

"Hello, Dr. Graham. I'm the assistant for Mr. Russell. Please follow me to conference room." The young woman led Dakota down one hallway, before turning around to go in the opposite direction. "I'm sorry. I'm new here and still getting lost."

The assistant opened the heavy oak door of the conference room. As Dakota entered the room, the buzz of the conversation seemed to stop suddenly and all heads turned toward her in unison. She felt her cheeks blaze with color.

A woman in a black Chanel suit walked over to Dakota, extending her hand. She was a classic beauty with her blond hair pulled back in a bun, a la Grace Kelly. The woman did not appear a day over fifty years old, although Dakota suspected some skillful plastic surgery had taken ten to fifteen years away.

As she shook Dakota's hand, the woman said, "I'm Candace Anderson, Fenton's wife. You must be the representative from the Broad Art Museum. Fenton had wonderful modern art pieces he wished to donate to your new venture."

Dakota was familiar with the new Eli and Edythe Broad Art Museum, with its glass and aluminum pleated exterior, currently being constructed at Michigan State University. Shaking her head, Dakota said, "No, I am not affiliated with the museum. To be quite honest with you, I don't know why I was invited to attend today. I do wish to extend my condolences for your loss, Mrs. Anderson."

A gray haired gentleman, standing at the head of a long, polished table, interrupted their conversation. "For those whom I have not met, I'm Arnold Russell, Mr. Anderson's personal attorney. If I could ask you all to have a seat, we can get started now that everyone is here."

Dakota counted nine seats, each with their own pad of paper and water bottle. She noted Candace took a seat next to Mr. Russell. Dakota chose a seat at the far end, sheltered from view by a large, burly man.

Mr. Russell continued, "Good afternoon and thank you for honoring the request of Mr. Fenton S. Anderson to hold a Reading of the Will. Fenton was one of our oldest and most valued clients. But more importantly, he was a personal friend of mine." Mr. Russell's voice waivered momentarily with emotion. "As you know, a Reading of the Will is not the customary protocol for disposition of property. Fenton always did have a flare for the dramatic," he softly chuckled.

Dakota looked around the group gathered at the table. The scenario felt like vultures hovering over a carcass. She eyed the door and wondered if she could escape. She was feeling very trapped.

Mr. Russell walked over to a large wall mounted flat screen televison, pulled out a CD from his jacket pocket and inserted the CD.

"Fenton had been more a man of action, than a man of words. But at the end of his life, Fenton felt the need to speak his mind, as well as his heart, to those important to him. So with that being said, let us begin hearing Fenton's last words."

Dakota watched the video screen come alive. The background was a cozy looking room, with wood paneling and hard wood floors. The centerpiece was a lovely field stone fireplace. An elderly man walked slowly, but stately, into the scene, assisted by a cane. He sat down on the granite hearth. Dakota thought he looked familiar, but could not place him. Despite his wrinkles and frailty, Dakota sensed he had been a handsome man in his day.

The man began speaking, "Thank you all for making time in your busy schedules to humor this old man's wishes. I, Fenton S. Anderson, being of sound mind and state, do proclaim this video will to be my true intention, nullifying all wills made before this. Ok, that takes care of Arnold's verbiage," he said with a wink. "You've been a great counselor and buddy, Arnold".

Dakota glanced around the table. Mr. Russell was pulling out his handkerchief. The others in the room looked as uncomfortable as she felt.

Fenton continued speaking, "Everyone here represents a part of my life I treasured. I'd like to start with the representative for the Eli and Edythe Broad Art Museum. You know, a wise woman once told me that I needed to figure out my passion in life. I graduated with an engineering degree from Michigan State College, which later became Michigan State University. But my true interests were my art classes. I have been privileged to acquire a wonderful modern art collection.

I hope the Broad Museum will accept my collection as a gift, to be displayed or sold, as they see fit. I regret I did not live to see the grand opening."

An African American woman nodded her head in acceptance as Mr. Russell handed her a thick catalog of Fenton's art collection.

"I also welcome my niece Michelle Anderson Pierce and nephew Philip Anderson Pierce. You know, I loved your mother, my sister, very much. I regret all the family get-togethers I was too busy to attend. I missed a lot of your lives growing up. I leave each of you $500,000.

Dakota noted the couple, who looked in their late sixties, sitting next to Candace. They seemed pleased with their new found money. Dakota's anxiety level was continuing to rise as she nervously swung her crossed leg under the table.

"Hey Walter, are you out there buddy?"shouted Fenton. Dakota jumped in her seat. The man shielding Dakota from the rest of the crowd yelled back, "Sure am, Fenton!"

"Walter Penske, my right hand at the Sanford and Augusta Anderson Foundation. You have done a bang up job managing the endowment and distributing the funds. You have dedicated your life to the foundation's mission of preserving Michigan's natural resources. You know, my family's fortune was made from harvesting Michigan's timber. The Anderson's will continue to give back to help replenish natural timber reserves, animal habitat, and safeguard Michigan's greatest asset, fresh clean water. Ten percent of the profits from Anderson Technologies will continue to fund the Foundation after my death."

"You're the best, Fenton!" proclaimed Walter, vigorously clapping. Noting that no one else was picking up the applause, Walter self consciously stopped clapping.

"I couldn't forget my secretary for the past forty-five years, Olivia Thompson. How can I thank you for your steadfast loyalty and patience with me? Please accept $100,000 as a token of my vast appreciation. Don't spend it all on your grand kids. Do the Greek Island Cruise you have dreamed about," said Fenton.

A woman sitting across from Dakota picked up her water bottle and toasted the television screen. "Godspeed, Fenton."

"Candace, my beautiful Candace...You were a wonderful hostess and helped clinch many a business deal over the years...You gave me the best gift ever in our son, Joel, and for this I will be eternally grateful..."

Dakota notice Candace looked radiant with the words of praise.

Fenton continued," I am sorry that I was not a better husband to you, and that I was not able to give you the love you deserved. I hope the next chapter in your life will be more satisfying for you. You will have our main house in White Hills, East Lansing; our winter home in Sanibel Island, Florida; and our summer home in Traverse City, Michigan. I will also direct that you receive a monthly payment of $50,000 from Anderson Technologies for the rest of your life.

Dakota saw Candace pale with the honesty of Fenton's words. This public display of emotion and regret went against Dakota's natural tendency to hold things close to the vest.

Only one other person besides Dakota remained unaddressed at the table. She surmised him to be Joel Anderson, the son of the deceased. Joel was average height, perhaps carrying a few extra pounds. His faded blond hair was closely cropped on the sides but on the crown, the hair was little longer and starting to curl. He had callused hands from manual work, not what she expected in a multimillionaire.

Fenton's voice drew her back to the screen. "Joel...a father could not be more proud of a son. You stand on integrity and honesty. Your intelligence is without question. But I worry about you, son...that you will grow old alone. I know your first marriage was a disaster...Lord knows, I was no example. I was old enough to be your grandfather, and I was absent too much of the time. But I treasured every minute we spent together..."

Dakota glanced at Joel. She could see a hint of his lower lip trembling. Surely Fenton's son would be the last person addressed, and she could silently exit soon.

Fenton continued, "Joel, I leave you controlling shares of Anderson Technologies and Anderson Research Center. I also place you as Chair of the Anderson Foundation. For all intent purposes, you have been handling these duties for years already...just don't get swallowed up by your career..."

Fenton looked down at his folded hands in his lap. The silence on the screen was dwarfed by the silence that hung in the room. Dakota knew in the pit of her stomach that her life was about to change forever.

Fenton looked up and spoke, "Dr. Dakota Graham... I am sure the others around the table are wondering why you are here today... Dakota, you are entitled to know your roots, and I know how you like to figure things out...Grace would be so proud of you..."

Dakota felt her arm pits wetting her shirt. Who was this Grace?

Fenton continued, "There are no do-over's in life. Oh, but if there were...Apologies don't changed things. All we can do is make peace with our God and move forward...which is what I have tried to do with my life. Dakota, I leave to you the contents of a safety deposit box at the Bank of Lansing...I guess it is now called Comerica Bank...in downtown Lansing. The contents include one key to the Hotel Kerns, some remarkable engineering drawings from 1934, and some vintage United States currency. The numismatist I consulted estimated these bills could bring in well over a million dollars due to their mint condition. "

Dakota heard gasps coming from the front of the table, in the direction of Candace, and the nephew. Dakota's hands and face felt numb from hyperventilating. Dakota was not cut out to be a millionaire. She was a struggling Family Practice doc, barely making payroll week to week. She must be about to be Punk'd.

Fenton continued talking, but Dakota could no longer concentrate. With shaky hands, she opened her water bottle and tried to quench her parched mouth. It was difficult to swallow. She was vaguely aware of Mr. Russell turning off the televison, talking about a written transcript that had been signed, and filing the document in the county clerk's office. All Dakota could think about was exiting the room.

Dakota stood up abruptly, bumping into Walter's chair. "Is everything okay, Dr. Graham?" asked Mr. Russell. Dakota did not stop to respond, and headed straight out the conference room door.

"Mother, do I have a sister you never told me about?" asked Joel.

"Oh, don't be fresh, Joel," Candace snapped.

As Joel arose and left the room, Candace walked over to the seat vacated by Dakota. She picked up Dakota's recapped water bottle, and slipped the bottle into her purse.

Philip Anderson, her nephew, wandered over to Candace and whispered, "What are you doing, sweetheart?"

Candace hissed back, "What does it look like I'm doing? I'm going to send this backwash in for DNA analysis and make sure that bitch is not Fenton's daughter. Then I'm going to move heaven and earth to make sure she never touches a nickel of his money."

Outside the Boji building, Dakota had already descended in the elevator and was bursting out on to the street. As she hustled down Allegan Street, she ran straight into a man walking towards her.

"Whoa, Dak. You look like you've seen a ghost!" It was Alex, reaching out to hold a trembling Dakota. "I was hoping to run into you, not literally, after your meeting....I thought you might need to talk."

"Alex, I am so confused. I just inherited over a million bucks from a man I've never even met before. And why is he leaving me a key to some hotel....the Hotel Kerns?" she asked.

"A million dollars? Congratulations!"

"No, it's not right. I don't deserve this money. There must be some mistake."

Alex put his arms around her waist and pulled Dakota tight against him. "I think the mistake is the name of the hotel. The Hotel Kerns burned down seventy-six years ago, just around the corner from here."

Dakota looked up at him. "How do you know this?"

"I've read about the hotel several times while researching histories of older buildings in Lansing. "

"Can you take me to the site?" asked Dakota.

As the two of them began walking east on Allegan, Candace and Philip exited the building as well. "Find out the name of the man walking with her, Philip," ordered Candace.

Dakota and Alex rounded the corner and headed a couple blocks away to Wentworth Park, at the corner of Michigan and Grand Avenues. The small corner park contained a clock carillon and a piece of twisted metal from the Twin Towers remains.

"We're here, "said Alex. "Come on over to the historical marker. "

Dakota had walked past this spot numerous times as her condominium was just down the street. But like so many busy Lansing residents, she had never stopped to read the words.

"It was a horrific fire, "said Alex. "Thirty-four people died trying to get out of the inferno. I read how people were jumping out of windows on to the street below or into the river behind the hotel in order to escape."

Alex continued to study the historical marker, with his arm wrapped around Dakota's waist. Next thing Alex knew, he was clutching a limp Dakota's body as she fainted in his arms.

SIX

Augusta Anderson was a woman on a mission as she walked quickly down Washington Avenue towards the Bank of Lansing. She was dressed in a gray wool coat with fur collar and matching fur hand muff. Her hat was tilted fashionably to the side, with her blond curls framing her face. She knew she could still turn heads at forty..

The limestone bank building was built three years ago. She smiled remembering how Fenton still was fascinated by the elephant statues and the mythical figures carved in the bank's arched doorway. She entered the bank, hoping to find Grace before she left for her lunch break.

As luck would have it, Grace was leaving the building at the same time and practically ran into Augusta. "Grace, just who I was looking for. Would you join me for lunch today?"

Normally Grace enjoyed visiting with her mother's best friend. But today, Grace was also a woman on a mission. Grace had a lunch date with a member of the Zonta Club at the Hotel Kerns cafeteria. "Mrs. Anderson, I would enjoy that so much, but unfortunately, I have a prior engagement."

"Grace, please call me Augusta. You're not a child anymore. Just give me a few minutes then."

Trying not to look impatient, Grace said, "My pleasure, Augusta."

"I have it on good authority that Fenton will be visiting you soon to ask you the favor of accompanying him to the J-Hop dance next month. It would mean the world to me if you would be his date for the evening."

The J-Hop was a formal dance held by the Junior Class at Michigan State College. Two years out of college and working full time, Grace felt a life time away from those co-eds. Furthermore, she did not want to encourage Fenton romantically.

"That is very flattering, but don't you think he would enjoy escorting one of his sister sorority members? "Grace asked.

"If you haven't figured out yet that Fenton thinks the sun rises and sets with you, then you are not as smart as I think you are. Now, I know finances are tight for you. We can go shopping together and pick out a wonderful gown—"

Grace interrupted, "Mr. Anderson and you have been so generous over the years. But I could not accept a new dress from you."

"Please don't break his heart, Grace. I know he has been so looking forward to this event."

A formal dress was definitely not in her budget, and would set the college fund back some. But she felt obligated to a family that had been so wonderful to her. "I would be honored to be his date, "Grace replied.

After a few amenities, the two women separated and Grace continued to walk quickly to the corner of Michigan and Grand Avenue. She rounded the corner to the north and entered the Hotel Kerns. Once in the lobby, she scouted the room for the woman she was meeting. She had phoned a Mrs. Curtis, a member of the Zonta Club, shortly after reading the article in the State Journal about the Club's mentoring goals. But the lobby looked full of business men and porters, with no one fitting Mrs. Curtis' self description.

Glancing at the wall clock, she realized only forty-five minutes remained of her lunch hour. She walked over to a porter and asked him if any messages had been left by a Mrs. Curtis. He directed her to the front desk, where Grace asked the same question. The man nodded. He said a message had been left, with regrets, but an illness had occurred in the family, and Mrs. Curtis would not be able to attend.

Grace thanked the man and walked back into the center of the lobby. She felt tears burn in her eyes. Despite all her hard work and unwavering determination, life seemed to throw one obstacle after another in her way.

Between skipping breakfast, and rushing to the appointment, she was beginning to feel light headed. As Grace felt the room spin, she felt strong arms encircle her. "Steady, Miss. You're as white as a ghost!"

She was helped over to a sofa against the wall. Grace looked up to see a kind and concerned face. His chestnut brown hair, parted on the side, partially covered one eye as he leaned over her. "Can I get you some water, Miss?" he asked.

"I am so embarrassed. I don't make it a habit to swoon into strange men's arms," she said with a smile.

"I'm only too happy to oblige. How about we get you a cup of strong coffee and some nourishment in the cafeteria down the hall?"

Grace glanced nervously at the clock again. Thirty-five minutes remained between now and getting a reprimand from her supervisor if she were late. But she knew she needed some food to finish the day. "I think that's a good idea."

The man reached down for her arm and steadied her as she rose and started walking. "I think I can manage now. Thank you for your assistance," said Grace.

The man continued to walk by her side. "I hear this is a popular watering hole in Lansing," he said. As they entered the cafeteria, she realized the place was packed. She was not going to find an empty seat, let alone get back to work on time. The man seemed to read her mind. "There are two empty seats at the end of that table. Why don't you sit down and let me get you a bowl of soup?"

Despite her independent streak, the table looked so inviting. "Thank you, sir. I think I will take you up on that offer."

"Two soups coming up and the name is Trevor, Trevor Moore." With that, he melted into the crowd.

Grace looked around her. The high walls were lined by white tiles, surrounded with a black tile border. Above the tiles, the walls were decorated by modern looking floral drawings. Her eyes drifted over to her knight in shining armor, walking towards her with a tray of food. He placed an inviting bowl of thick chicken and dumplings in front of her.

"Mr. Moore, are you traveling through Lansing?" Grace asked, as she crumbled crackers in her soup and started eating.

"Two months ago, I was lunching at Café de la Paix in Paris. Now I'm here at this lovely café at the Hotel Kerns....Mademoiselles in Paris don't hold a candle to the women in Lansing," Trevor said with a smile.

"And may I ask what brings a world traveler to our hamlet?" asked Grace between spoonfuls.

"I guess you could say I'm coming home again...I lied about my age at seventeen and enlisted in the Great War. My family had all died by that time, and it seemed the thing to do....I settled in Italy after the War and started a new family there. Now they are all gone as well, so I figured it was time to come home again."

Dakota had to finish swallowing before she could speak. "I lost my family at sixteen. I can't imagine repeating that loss again so soon."

"Enough about me. I'm sure you have an interesting story to tell," said Trevor.

Grace glanced up at the wall clock and jumped up suddenly. Five minutes remained before her supervisor Mr. Edgar would have new ammunition. "Oh my goodness! I need to run before I get fired. Thank you for the company, Mr. Moore." She reached in her pocket and placed thirty-five cents on the table. "I believe this will cover my meal. Safe travels, Mr. Moore." And with that, she sprinted out of the room.

"Wait! What's your name? " called Trevor, jumping up to follow her. A large group of garrulous business men entered the cafeteria at the same time. Trevor pushed through the group, running back towards the lobby, and out on to the street. But by then, she was gone. He heard a bell tower ringing at the top of the hour,, and he felt like the Prince, watching his Cinderella slip away.

SEVEN

Ann Arbor, Michigan
Wednesday, September 15, 2010
12:45pm

He could smell autumn today, his favorite season. The smell always reminded Dr. Peter Cho of returning to school. As he paced in the parking lot of Souviens, a startup company in Ann Arbor, he noticed the first hint of color changing in the leaves. He could even hear the distant sounds of the marching band practicing for The University of Michigan, his Alma Mater.

When he had been a graduate student here, choices had seemed either right or wrong, with the correct pathway clearly marked. But the older he became, the more he became a fretter, as his wife affectionately called him. When Dakota had phoned him to arrange a consult with Dr. Theo Everett, Dr. Cho had originally been eager for a second opinion on this baffling case. But the more Dr. Cho thought of this path, the more pitfalls he began to see.

On one hand, Dr. Everett was clearly a brilliant scientist. By fifteen years old, he was attending an Ivy League College. By the time he was twenty years old, he was working on his doctorate. On the other hand, his career had been rocky. He had failed to make tenure at Harvard and Stanford. It wasn't simply that his theories were controversial, but rather his tactics and interpersonal skills were often called into question.

Dr. Cho worried that the wrong step at this critical junction could set Dakota back...which is why he insisted on joining her for this consultation. He looked up to see her Saturn Hybrid turning into the lot. He walked over as she climbed out of her car.

As they shook hands, Dakota said, "Dr. Cho, thanks so much for coming all this way."

The pair walked towards the Souviens office building. The six story brick edifice did not offer a hint of what was inside. There were only long, narrow windows running along the ceiling of each floor. It was not until they entered the lobby entrance that Dr. Cho realized the building was built around a large garden area, with tall trees that predated the building. The walls around this arboretum were glass. Employees walking down the hallways not only could see the beauty of nature, but could also see their colleagues on the other sides of the building.

After notifying the security desk of their arrival, Dr. Cho walked over to the waiting area, and picked up a glossy prospectus on Souviens. He thought of the French word, souviens, meaning remember. Despite the remarkable advances in medicine in the twentieth century, understanding memory was still in its infancy as the twenty-first century began.

Opening the prospectus, he read about the research Souviens was conducting on developing a vaccine to prevent Alzheimer's disease. The vaccine would target the buildup of amyloid-beta plaque in the brain, believed to be one of the culprits in the devastating disease. Previous vaccine attempts by others had caused dangerous inflammatory reactions in the brain during human trials. Souviens felt its vaccine had addressed this issue. So far, the research had been funded by the company founders, but now Venture Capital firms were being pursued to take the research to the next level. The principle investigators and research scientists were listed, with short biographical information on each.

Dr. Cho had yet to read any references to Dr. Everett. He continued to browse through the pages until he reached a short section entitled Fundamental Research. Apparently Souviens had a small group of people doing pure research into understanding memory, both on how a memory is created and stored, and how it is lost. Dr. Everett was mentioned, among a handful of others. Souviens must be hoping that a proprietary discovery could be a bridge to a commercial success.

Dr. Cho's concentration was broken when he heard footsteps walking quickly toward them. He looked up to recognize Dr. Everett, dressed in a white lab jacket. Dr. Cho guessed that Dr. Everett was in his early sixties, with a tall, thin build, and only sparse silver hair remaining.

Dr. Everett zeroed in on Dakota and held out his hand. "I've been very anxious to talk with you, Dr. Graham. Please, follow me."

The group entered a small conference room just off the lobby, and they sat down at a round table. "So, Dr. Graham, fill me in on your memories," Dr. Everett said in a tone more akin to a command than a request. Apparently Dr. Everett was not much for small talk, thought Dr. Cho.

Dakota replied, "These aren't memories...They are more like dreams or visions of something I've never seen before—"

Dr. Everett interrupted, "I'll be the judge of that. Now start from the beginning."

Dakota replayed her history, starting with the death of her parents and brother in a car accident, followed by the recurrent sensory images of a burning building and carnage. During her story, Dr. Everett took detailed notes in a log book.

She took a deep breath and continued, "I have new information that I haven't had a chance to share even with Dr. Cho. Recently, I inherited a safety deposit box from a man I didn't know. One of the contents was a room key to the Hotel Kerns, a Lansing hotel that burned down in 1934, killing thirty-four people. A friend of mine was familiar with its history and took me to the site of the fire. Reading the historical marker...standing there, looking at the river ....somehow everything started to click, and I had this overwhelming feeling that this tragedy was somehow related to my dreams—"

Dr. Everett interrupted again, "You must stop looking into this matter. It's imperative to our research that you don't contaminate your memory with new facts. Now let's talk about what our research protocol will be—"

Now it was Dr. Cho's turn to interrupt. "Let's hold on for a moment here. We never said anything about Dakota being involved in any type of research. We only signed up for some conversations between colleagues." Dr. Cho had a protective streak towards his patients, and he was sensing potential exploitation. "Before we go any further, I need to hear more about your research."

Dr. Everett's face reddened as he turned to face Dr. Cho squarely. "I hardly need to prove my research acumen to a doctor that spends his days talking psychobabble to people on a couch!"

"Gentleman, please. Let's start over. Does your research have any bearing on my experiences?" Dakota redirected.

Dr. Everett needed a few minutes to collect his thoughts before answering. Dr. Cho recognized this personality type, having such a fragile sense of self worth that small perceived slights set off strong emotions.

Dr. Everett began his explanation, "Have you heard of the field of epigenetics?" As the others shook their heads no, he continued, "The best way to explain this may be to start with our Biology 101 course. We were all taught that inheritance comes from the DNA in our 23 pairs of chromosomes. A chromosome from each pair comes from Mom and Dad. "

This time the others nodded in agreement. He continued, "Turns out this in not the full story. Every cell in our body has the same DNA in it....But how does a heart cell know how to beat and a stomach cell know how to digest food? As the embryo divides, cells turns off the majority of their genes, with only the genes unique to its eventual destination left on. Clearly what genes are turned on or off inside a cell has major ramification for an organism. This is an example of epigenetics, inheritance that is not simply due to the order of the DNA sequence. "

"So is this process of switching genes off and on predetermined for a species or do parental experiences have some impact on which genes are active in their offspring?" asked Dakota.

"You are asking a perceptive question, Dr. Graham. We are discovering that what occurs in the life of a parent, both the mother and the father, has bearing on the offspring... Let me give you an example of a fascinating study out of Duke University. "

Dr. Everett walked over to a cabinet and pulled out some photographs. He placed the first one on the table and said, "Here is a female Agouti mouse...This breed is usually yellow and very obese, and will most likely develop diabetes. Now if we feed this mother a diet rich in Vitamin B12, folic acid and choline around the time of conception, here is her prodigy." He placed another photograph down, showing a thin, brown mouse. "What's more, this brown mouse will most likely be free of diabetes and continue to have healthy prodigy, all due to her mother's diet."

"Is it only the maternal experiences that can cause this epigenetic effect?" said Dakota.

"No, we are now realizing that fathers can also have epigenetic effects on their offspring as well. Just recently, a study out of The University of New South Wales examined genetically thin male rats that were fed a high fat diet. These rats were then mated with slender female rats. The daughter rats developed obesity and glucose problems as they aged. Their on/off switches in the pancreas, where insulin is made, were found to be in the wrong position... Dad's habits, not his DNA, determined the fate of his daughters. "

"With the obesity epidemic facing us in this country, can you imagine the potential health benefits if this research translates into human biology? "asked Dr. Cho.

"Souviens definitely sees the potential commercial benefit... which is why my unit has continued to be funded."

"How do cells remember what genes are to be turned on and off?" asked Dr. Cho.

"Cellular memory...That is precisely the area of my research at Souviens...We know that by attaching a chemical compound called a methyl group to a gene, it will be silent. But how does a sperm or an egg direct which genes are to be inactivated in the embryo? And how does a cell remember after cellular division which genes are to be methylated? "

The three doctors sat silently for a few moments, mulling over the information being discussed. The silence was interrupted by a knock at the door, with the receptionist poking her head into the room. "Dr. Everett, just a reminder from the top that the representatives from the

Gremald Group will be arriving in about 30 minutes." And with that, she slipped away.

Dr. Everett's face crinkled in frustration. "That's our latest Venture Capital group that I will need to do a dog and pony show for..."

Dakota did not want to leave without some answers to her original question. "Dr. Everett, I understand how busy you are, and I really appreciate the time you have given us today. But I'm still confused how my experiences relate to your research."

Dr. Everett walked over to the door that was still ajar, and quietly closed it. He turned and looked directly at Dakota. "What I have described to you so far is my day job, so to speak. However, in the evenings and on weekends, I have my own investigations underway, research that I have not shared with anyone prior to today."

A chill went up Dr. Cho's spine as Dr. Everett continued to speak. "I believe that human memories can be transmitted through subsequent generations, aided by this epigenetic process. One of your ancestors lived the very experience that you are seeing in your so called dreams. And if you will work with me, I think the two of us can unlock a mystery that will rock the very foundations of our scientific knowledge!"

Dakota was at a loss of words. She glanced over at Dr. Cho, who had a concerned look on his face. This man may be the biggest quack around, or he may be a genius. But in the depths of her being, his words seemed to ring true.

"How do we start?" she asked.

"With your genealogy, "he replied.

Dakota smiled and said, "I know just the cousin to introduce you to...."

EIGHT

Fenton had the young man pinned up against the wall, and spoke very deliberatively. "Benny, I don't care that we've been friends since grammar school or that you're my fraternity brother ...If you ever speak disrespectfully about Grace again, I will kill you."

"Easy, pally. I didn't mean no harm. But you gotta admit...You'd have a better chance for some...fun...if you had asked one of those sweet co-eds that swarm around you to the J-Hop instead of Grace. Sure, Grace is pretty enough, but you gotta admit that she's boring... always talking about college or Roosevelt or turmoil in Europe. She's like talking to my parents!"

Fenton released Benny and walked toward the sink in their room. "She has intelligence, Benny, something you seem to have lost tonight. Now get ready, and so help me, you better not ruin tonight for me."

Benny reached into his suit coat jacket and pulled out a silver flask. "Here, have a little hooch, Fen. You're entirely too tense tonight."

Fenton looked at the flask for a moment, and then grabbed it out of Benny's hand. "Tense, thanks to you...I guess a little swig couldn't hurt anything."

The two men finished getting dressed in silence. Fenton surveyed himself in the mirror and was pleased with the end results. Students traditionally were dressed to the nines at the J-Hop dance, hosted annually by the Junior Class at Michigan State College. His new black suit was the latest style. It had broad shoulders, a high waist line, and wide pants that were tapered at the cuff. It was accented by a white vest and white bow tie. Whether it was his image or the whiskey taking hold, he felt warmth growing inside that was dissipating his anxiety.

They grabbed their top coats and hats, and headed out into the bitter February air. Fenton was anxious to show off his new car to Grace. His father had surprised him last month with a Reo Flying Cloud four door sedan. Other fathers gave gifts when their sons were making them proud. Sanford gave gifts as motivation when Fenton had disappointed him, such as his recent college performance.

But Fenton loved the car, with its curved wheel covers and the horizontal side vents that gave the car a sleek look. He especially liked that the bulky gear box was gone between the passenger and the driver. He imagined Grace snuggled up against him, touring the countryside.

The men climbed into the Reo and headed down the side street to Michigan Avenue which would take them the few miles from East Lansing to the boarding house on Hillsdale Street in Lansing. As they pulled into the driveway, Benny said to Fenton, "One more swig to calm your nerves, Casanova." Fenton tipped the flask quickly and gulped the whiskey down.

He walked up to the front door of the home. It was a large white two story Colonial, with green shutters, dating from around the turn of the century. Several additions for boarders had been built on to the original structure, including Grace's room in the back, which had its own entrance as well.

Before Fenton could ring the bell, Charles Mann opened the door, with Louise following closely behind him. Fenton was greeted by the ever present aroma of cinnamon from Louise's constant baking. The trio exchanged pleasantries as he walked into the spacious front parlor.

Fenton caught his breath as he spotted Grace entering the room. Her black velvet dress closely hugged her petite body until it flared out near the hemline. The front neckline had a wide band of contrasting gray fabric, with just a gentle scoop to the collar bone in the front. But then the neck line plunged over her shoulders to her mid back, ending in a bow. Her short sleeves looked like a small cape over her shoulders.

Fenton knew from his mother that Grace had never been to a formal dance before. Rumor had it that Charles had been schooling Grace in the waltz and the fox trot to the music of the Victor Young Orchestra on her Philco radio. He also knew that her dress, purchased at Arbaugh's Department Store, cost a pretty penny with her tight budget.

He felt touched that she had done all these things for him. It only made the love he felt for her since he was a young boy grow. Grace still looked at him as a younger brother. But while he lacked confidence in his academic ability, he was pretty sure of his charm with the ladies. It was just a matter of time before Grace would see that they were meant to be together.

"You're a vision of loveliness tonight, Grace, "said Fenton.

"Why thank you, kind sir. You're pretty dapper yourself."

The pair said their goodbyes and walked out, arm in arm towards his car. "Oh Fenton, Reo certainly is making exquisite automobiles. It's a shame that the company is struggling in this depression, as is the rest of our country...A family friend told me that the number of cars produced is only ten percent of the production from when my father worked at Reo, "said Grace as Fenton opened the door for her to climb into the front seat.

"Good evening, Benny. Nice to see you again," said Grace to the passenger in the back seat.

Benny replied, "Same here."

Fenton jumped in the driver seat and started the engine. "Grace, your father would have been intrigued with this car. It has a patented self shifter mechanism, first of its kind. I can keep both hands on the wheel and not worry about shifting between gears."

Benny poked his head between them and said, "Now you two love birds can hold hands while driving."

"Settle down, Benny," cautioned Fenton.

The rest of the drive was spent in small talk as they picked up Benny's date and headed for their destination, the Lansing Masonic Temple. The place was already hopping by their arrival. Despite the bad economy, there was a very good turnout of students for the affair. The evening was going just as Fenton had dreamed. The event began with a large banquet, with several courses of delicious food. The conversation at their table of six was light hearted, discussing recent movies, radio shows and the upcoming sports season at MSC. Even Benny seemed charming and on his best behavior.

The dinner ended with the class leaders offering several toasts, followed by the Grand March. All of the ticket holders formed a procession around the large ballroom with well dressed, stylish co-eds. Those who could not afford the pricey tickets lined the mezzanine balcony to look down upon the elegant performance. Once everyone was assembled, a large group photo was taken. Fenton made sure that he and Grace were near the front as he wanted a photograph to remember this night forever.

Then the dancing began, to the music of the Ted Weem's Band. Fenton was proud that his class had obtained a well known radio artist for the J-Hop. As he and Grace moved around the dance floor, he held her tight, as a man held a woman, not as a brother and sister. Grace seemed to be glowing, and he felt she was responding to him.

So what was wrong with his sneaking a few swigs of whiskey throughout the night? This was a celebration, and he saw no harm in imbibing some spirits to add sparkle to the night. The girls were heading off to the powder room, and Fenton thought this would be a good time to find his flask again. He headed back to their table where his top coat was draped over the chair. He pulled the flask out of his pocket, closed his eyes, and took a nice, slow drink, enjoying the warmth in his throat.

He felt someone touch his arm, and he opened his eyes to see Grace standing closely beside him. She spoke softly. "Fenton, we are having such a lovely time tonight. Do you really need to drink more whiskey?"

Benny stepped up from behind Grace and took the flask from Fenton. "Prohibition has ended, Grace. You teetotalers lost. Fen here is just trying to have some fun. Leave him alone."

"Back off, Benny. This is a private conversation," snarled Fenton. "Grace, here's a fact for you. Did you read in the Lansing State Journal that the State of Michigan has already made over two million dollars on the sale of beer since being legalized last May? That's a lot of money to benefit the good people of our state." Benny smiled as he enjoyed being the professorial one for a change.

"Fenton, I hear the band starting to play one of my favorite songs," Grace hinted. Fenton stood up, a little unevenly, offered his arm to Grace, and escorted her into the crowd. After a couple turns around dance floor, Grace spoke, "Your sister tells me you have been missing a lot of classes lately and have failed a couple exams. I'm worried alcohol is playing a part."

Fenton looked over Grace's shoulder at the other couples dancing. He couldn't look her in the eye, and deny the situation.

"It feels like we've known each other forever. You can tell me if something is bothering you..."

"Sometimes I feel like I'm expected to be something I'm not. I have pretty big shoes to fill, following Sanford Anderson." As soon as the words slipped out, Fenton was embarrassed to look so weak.

Grace smiled up at him and said, "No one can replace Sanford. But you don't have to. You're a force on to your own. You have warmth and a wit that can light up a room. And you are very creative. You just need to find your passion in life."

Fenton felt flushed by her praise. "My passion is you, Grace," he said, slightly slurred.

"It's a lot of pressure to put on a person to be the source of your passion in life. People die, or change...or leave for medical school... You need to find happiness from within. What really excites you?"

Fenton concentrated on the dance steps for awhile. He was beginning to have trouble thinking of two things at the same time. Then he said something that surprised even himself. "I love art... sculptures, paintings...Can't make a living with that, though."

Grace replied, "That may be true, but your love of art can make you excited about life. Even your engineering courses can be seen as a study of art....the lines of a structure, the interplay of parts together... And I bet if you raised your grades, your Dad would let you take a course in art history at MSC. "

They finished dancing in silence, thinking of their discussion. As they were leaving the dance floor, Benny tapped Fenton's shoulder.

"Hey, Fen, would you mind if me and my date hitched a ride home with some other folks? There's an after party happening that we'd like to check out."

This could not be more perfect, thought Fenton. He bid Benny goodnight and went to retrieve Grace's wrap. The dancing was starting to thin out, and this seemed like the perfect time to escort Grace home.

Fenton left first to pull his car in front of the Temple as a light snow began to fall. Once they were both in the car, Grace said, "Fenton, thank you so much for asking me to the J-Hop. Dancing is so much fun, and you were a good sport when I stepped on your toe. I had a wonderful time." Fenton returned her smile, and reached over to hold her hand.

Fenton loved the drive home. The snow was coating all the trees with white powdered sugar, and the world seemed magical, with Grace's hand nestled in his. Fenton's only concern was that he may have overdone the whiskey. Although he took pride in holding his liquor, he usually didn't combine alcohol with three courses of rich food. His gut was rumbling a little, but he willed those thoughts out of his mind. Instead his mind drifted to thoughts of kissing Grace good night.

They arrived back at the boarding house, and he pulled the Reo into the driveway. A front light had been left on for Grace, but the rest of the windows looked dark. "I think I'll let myself in through my private door so I don't wake up the Manns or the other boarders, " said Grace. Fenton liked the idea of the more private doorway for their goodbyes.

He turned the engine off and climbed out of the Reo. The ground seemed to be moving. He closed his eyes tightly for a moment, hoping the vertigo sensation would leave. Upon opening his eyes, the world looked a little steadier, and he walked around to open the door for Grace. She took one look at his pale face and said, "Fenton, are you all right?"

He swallowed hard the bile that was trying to move up into his throat. "Everything is fine, Grace. "

He took her arm a little clumsily, and they walked around the house to her back entrance. His perfect speech that he had prepared seemed to have slipped his mind. What was it again...something about giving him a chance to prove his love and worthiness for her... Grace was speaking, but he wasn't quite catching the words. Was this the time to give her the tender kiss that made other girls swoon?

Fenton decided to make his move. His hands didn't seem to move smoothly as he wrapped his arm around her waist. Warmth spread over him, but this time, it didn't seem pleasant. He suddenly felt sweaty and dizzy, not from love, but from nausea. Before he could stop, he felt his stomach contents moving into his mouth. He reflexively bent over, violently vomiting, with emesis spraying all over the snow and the hemline of Grace's new evening dress.

He wanted to curl up and die.

NINE

Lansing, Michigan
Thursday, September 16, 2010
11:45 AM

"And to your left is the Thomas L. Cooley Law School. This limestone neoclassic building was originally built in 1923 as the Lansing Masonic Temple. Now it has been transformed into part of the nation's largest law school."

Alex Zahn felt like a tour guide, as he chauffeured a potential investor around. Never mind his pride. What was important was securing capital to start his business over again. He turned off Capitol Avenue, onto Kalamazoo Street and onto Grand Avenue to show off Lansing's most impressive renovation project.

"To your right is the old Board of Water and Light plant which powered Lansing for decades. Doomed for demolition, this beautiful Art Deco step back structure has been given new life as it is being transformed into the new Accident Funds Insurance Headquarters. Note how the structure has multiple colors of brick, from purple near the bottom, to red and orange in the middle to yellow at top, to represent the stages of coal combustion. This project is a catalyst to many new business ventures downtown."

Alex glanced at his passenger. The man was definitely uninterested in the history and architecture of Lansing, instead glancing frequently at his Blackberry.

"Old buildings that are rehabilitated and updated preserve crafts-manship and beauty that cannot be duplicated today, and fit with the green movement of recycling and reusing. "

Now the man had his eyes closed. Alex was surely losing this sale. Stick with the bottom line, Alex chided himself. The man just wants to diversify his portfolio with real estate and could care less about the esthetics or the morals.

Alex circled around the block back towards Michigan Avenue. He caught sight of the historical marker where Dakota had fainted in his arms. That room key to the old burned down hotel was certainly puz-zling.....But Alex was sure the key to his future was Dakota. If he could only break though the protective walls that she had put up around her... She had been so preoccupied since the reading of the will that he had only talked to her on the phone.

But now, he needed to focus on the matter at hand. Jump starting his failed career was step one to getting his life back on track. He had planned to take the man to lunch at Clara's, a charming old railroad depot remodeled into a restaurant. Instead, he decided to head for the brand new Troppo's.

"I think I'll be able to convince you over lunch that my renovation project would afford you a wonderful return on your investment, with tax incentives for brown field redevelopment and historic preservation." Now the man was looking interested. Remember, in the end, money is the true key, Alex told himself.

TEN

Lansing, Michigan
Monday, February 19, 1934
9:30am

Trevor Moore looked out his fourth floor room at the Hotel Kerns on to Grand Avenue, and reflected on the convoluted path that had brought him to this spot. He remembered the excitement of going off to war in 1917, how it had been an antidote to the emptiness he felt after losing his family. Of course, the naivety of youth could not have prepared him for the carnage he witnessed in the Great War. He eventually became a member of the sole American regiment that participated in the Italian Vittorio Veneto offensive that ended the war on the Italian front. Within days of their victory against the Austrians, the Armistice ending the war had been signed as well.

At loose ends, Trevor had followed one of the Italian soldiers back to his home in the Po River Valley of Northern Italy. Little did Trevor know at the time how this decision would change his life forever, giving him another chance at love and family.

Trevor walked away from the window and tried to shake off the wave of pain. Thoughts of his wife Pia still caused a deep visceral ache that was no less acute today than the day she died nine years ago. He still remembered his first encounter with the cousin of his Italian army buddy. She was not beautiful in the Hollywood sense of the word, but her sparkling intellect and fiery personality had attracted him from the start.

When he married Pia, he also gained a father-in-law, Aberto, who would become the father Trevor had never known. Trevor's own father was a traveling salesman, mostly absent from home, even when in town. After five of the happiest years of his life, what should have been a wonderful event tore his world apart when Pia started bleeding early in her pregnancy, and passed away. He stayed on with Aberto, bonded by their grief.

Aberto was a successful industrialist, from a wealthy Italian family. He was also an ingenious inventor. The two of them often worked into the night, perfecting Aberto's experiments and designs. Now Trevor found himself in Lansing, working on fulfilling the three promises he had made on Aberto's death bed.

Trevor pulled on his top coat, making sure his leather pouch was safely tucked into his interior coat pocket. He guarded the pouch with his life, never leaving without it. Grabbing his fedora, he ventured out onto the streets. His first stop was the Bank of Lansing just around the corner from the Hotel Kerns. Since his arrival in Lansing a couple weeks ago, he had been getting the lay of the land. It was time to start making connections, and that required some cash on hand.

As Trevor was walking towards the bank, he thought of all the poor souls who had lost their entire life savings in bank collapses over the past several years. Trevor had been raised not to trust banks. After the death of his last parent, it took weeks to collect the family's savings that had been squirreled away in the nooks and crannies of their home. Now his bank was a small silver box, nestled safely in his pouch.

However, he needed money for the next stage of his plan. The Hotel Kerns was a prime watering hole for legislators away from home and buying a few rounds at the bar was a good ice breaker for future business relationships. He was running low on small denomination bills and needed to break a $500 note.

Trevor entered the lobby and looked around. There were two bank teller windows in use. One was occupied by an older man whose scowl looked permanently engraved on his face. The other window, to his surprise and delight, was occupied by his Cinderella. Their brief encounter had made a lasting impression on him. Despite her petite frame, he sensed a strength and determination in her that he found intriguing. She was currently busy helping someone, so he placed himself in line.

When it was his turn, he saw a flicker of a smile on her face. "Good morning, Mr. Moore. How may I help you today?" she asked.

Trevor kept his voice low, pleased she remembered him, but sensing the curmudgeon could cause trouble if Trevor obviously flirted with his Cinderella. "Mademoiselle, it's wonderful to see you again. You left so quickly from the café that I wasn't able to ask you your name."

Trevor could sense she was uncomfortable so he returned to the matter at hand. "I have a $500 note that I need to exchange for smaller bills. Would I be able to do that?"

"Do you have an account here at Bank of Lansing?" she asked.

"Truthfully, I'm leery of banks. I'm more comfortable with storing money in mattresses."

She chuckled softly then said, "Perhaps being in Europe you didn't hear about the newly created Federal Deposit Insurance Corporation. President Roosevelt created this agency to protect depositors up to $2500. "

"Is there a problem, Miss Dunning?" The curmudgeon had left his window and walked over to her area.

"I was just explaining to Mr. Moore about the FDIC, Mr. Edgar," she said.

"I apologize, Mr. Moore. This is not her area of expertise. Please allow me to introduce you to our bank manager."

Trevor wanted to punch this man in the nose. Instead, Trevor decided to put him in his place. "Actually, Miss Dunning is quite a sales person. I have decided to open an account today due to her reassurances."

The curmudgeon pointed across the lobby. "Our bank manager will be happy to help you, Mr. Moore."

There was nothing Trevor could do at that point. He had backed himself into opening an account, and still had not had a chance to learn more about his Cinderella. As he walked away, he heard the curmudgeon talking low, but threatening to Miss Dunning.

"It's bad enough that you're taking a job away from our unemployed men that need to support their families. Now you are overstepping your duties. You're only here because old man Anderson is one of our biggest depositors. But I have my eye on you, Grace. "

Her face flushed, but she kept her gaze steady and her spine straight. Trevor felt a sense of admiration, as well as protectiveness, all at the same time. He knew he would be returning for another encounter with the lovely Grace.

ELEVEN

Mason, Michigan
Saturday, September 25, 2010
10:30 AM

Morgan peered again through the curtain, looking for her anticipated guest. Dakota had been uncharacteristically vague when
explaining the purpose of the man's visit--something to do with investigating possible connections between Dakota and this Fenton Anderson
who had made her cousin Lansing's newest millionaire. Morgan also did
not understand why Dakota was not joining them for this consultation.
Again, only a vague explanation had been offered.

Morgan's mother Charity had been invited for this session as well.
Charity was consumed with playing with her twin grandsons since her
arrival, so Morgan had not yet updated her mother on Dakota's windfall.

Finally, a Toyota pulled into her driveway, and Dr. Theo Everett
stepped out, briefcase in tow. Morgan felt a small chill. Nothing came
for free, particularly a million dollars. She worried Dakota may have
unexpected consequences with this inheritance.

Morgan opened the door and invited Dr. Everett into her large reno-
vated farmhouse. She and her husband had fallen in love with the hundred year old beauty, complete with a partially wooded ten acre lot. The
acreage allowed her boys and dogs lots of room to burn off energy.

Dr. Everett followed her into a wide open kitchen with a large
wooden table. She had spread out much of her genealogy research before

his arrival. She called her mother to join them, and made the necessary introductions.

Morgan said, "I need to bring my mother up to speed, Dr. Everett, as she has been out of town for awhile. Mother, Dakota was invited to a Reading of a Will for a wealthy industrialist whom she did not know. For no apparent reason, the deceased left Dakota over a million dollar inheritance."

"Is this some kind of prank, Morgan? You and Dakota had fertile imaginations growing up, and I succumbed to more than one hoax," Charity chuckled.

"No, Mother, this is serious. Dakota has asked Dr. Everett to help her figure out why a stranger has bequeathed her money." Morgan held her tongue and did not ask her burning question. Why was this educated scientist interested in poking around their family tree?

Dr. Everett also held his tongue. It was obvious Morgan and Charity knew nothing about Dakota's dreams and the possible connection to the Hotel Kern's fire. He was quite pleased about their ignorance of the matter. This allowed for better data collection, with less contamination of their memory by conjecture.

"I would be very happy for Dakota if this were true. She has worked hard all her life, put herself through school, and is still struggling with student loans. But the circumstances seem suspicious to me. Who is this benefactor?" asked Charity.

"A man named Fenton Anderson. Does that name mean anything to you, Charity?" Dr. Everett asked.

Charity blanched. "Mother, are you ok? You look like you've seen a ghost." Morgan was concerned. Her sixty-six year old mother who still ran in 5K races suddenly looked frail and weak.

Dr. Everett studied Charity carefully. "Tell us what you remember, Charity. "

"I haven't heard that name since I was a little girl. But I remember like it was yesterday. I was playing with my sister, Charlotte, nine years my senior, in our front parlor. The door bell rang, and my mother answered it. She was normally such a calm, unflustered woman. But when she returned, she looked worried. She shooed us upstairs, and told us to sit quietly in our room until she came for us. Then she allowed a man into our home."

Charity arose and poured herself a glass of water from the tap.

Morgan walked over to her and placed an arm on Charity's shoulder. "What does this have to do with the name Fenton Anderson?"

Charity turned around and looked at Dr. Everett. "While we were up in our room, I could hear my mother talking to a man. The voices seemed raised and emotional. But I couldn't make out the words. Later, after he left, my mother joined us on our bed. While she was talking to both of us, I had the sense her words were directed more to Charlotte than to me...She said if we were ever approached by a man named Fenton Anderson, we were not to talk to him, or go anywhere with him. It scared the stuffing out of me."

"Did you ever see him or hear his name again?" Dr. Everett asked.

"No, I never heard his name mentioned again until this afternoon," answered Charity.

"Let's move on. I would like to review the information you have gathered about Dakota's maternal lineage, "said Dr. Everett.

"Dakota and I share our maternal lineage. But I also have lots of interesting stories of her father's ancestors—"

Dr. Everett interrupted, "I'm only interested in learning about her maternal lineage. Now, if you would start with her mother--"

"But how do you know that her father's history is not pertinent?" asked Morgan.

"I am the investigator. Thus, I ask the questions. Please, let's get back to the matter at hand," Dr. Everett snapped.

Morgan wanted to boot this arrogant man out the door, but she would put up with him for Dakota's sake...at least for the time being.

"Dakota's mother was born Eliza Bennett. Eliza is actually my first cousin, but due to the gap in ages between my mother and her sister Charlotte, my age is actually closer to my second cousin, Dakota," said Morgan as she handed him a photograph of Eliza taken in her mid twenties.

"Eliza and her husband were archeologists. Although they were professors at Michigan State University, they spent a lot of time at archeological digs around the world. Often they would take Dakota, and eventually her younger brother Niles, with them."

"Tell me about their deaths, "Dr. Everett directed.

Charity picked up the story at this point. "When Dakota was eight years old, my niece Eliza received an award from an Archeology Society in Washington, DC. Dakota's second grade class had a field trip planned the same week, and she was upset about missing the activity. So my sister Charlotte, Dakota's grandmother, offered to babysit. Dakota's parents and her younger brother were killed in an automobile accident on the way home from DC. "

"And Dakota's reaction to the news?" he asked.

"She was inconsolable. She didn't eat or sleep well for months. In fact, she suffered from nightmares and chronic insomnia for some time, "said Charity.

"Now you say there was a large age gap between you and your sister Charlotte... not the usual family pattern in that time period..." he said.

"I suspect my parents had fertility problems, but those matters were never discussed back in the day...My sister Charlotte was born in 1935, when my mother was thirty-one. I was born nine years later when my mother was forty."

Dr. Everett perked up when he heard the date 1935. "What day was Charlotte born?" His heart was pounding with excitement. "September first," said Charity.

"Do you remember Charlotte's birth weight? Was she a full term baby?" asked Dr. Everett, as he tried to calculate date of conception in his head.

"How can my Aunt Charlotte's birth weight have any bearing on the matter on hand?" Morgan asked, with a not too subtle irritation in her voice.

But Dr. Everett was like a dog after a bone, and was oblivious to Morgan's suspicions. "Her date of conception is very important. Do you have a baby book for Charlotte?"

"Ok, this is getting too weird. I need to know what the devil you are looking for, Dr. Everett. I have documents detailing Dakota's lineage all the way back to England. I even obtained cheek swabs from both of us for DNA testing to send into the National Geographic Genographic Study...See, these maps show our distant ancestors' migrations from Africa into Europe....And you're fixated on a baby weight!"

Dr. Everett shook his head in disgust. People had such limited scientific knowledge. "Sending in cheek swabs from both you and Dakota was a waste of money. These types of tests in female subjects track mitochondrial DNA. Mitochondrial DNA is inherited solely from ones mother. Since you and Dakota have a common maternal ancestor, namely Charity's and Charlotte's mother, your mitochondrial DNA would be the same."

"I don't know anything about Mitochondrial DNA, Dr. Everett. But you are wrong about the two samples being a waste of money. Look how these documents trace Morgan's ancestors migrating to Northern Europe and Dakota's ancestors settling in the Mediterranean regions," said Charity.

Dr. Everett grabbed the reports and studied them carefully. "Morgan, either you sent in the wrong samples....or you and Dakota are not related."

Morgan slammed her hands down on the table, spewing papers at the same time, and jumped to her feet, "That does it...I want you out of my house. I don't know what type of con you are trying to perpetuate, Dr. Everett, but we are done here."

"Facts don't lie, Morgan. These reports list the tested sequence of your Mitochondrial DNA...They are significantly different from Dakota's. And look at these photographs....You and Charity-- tall, blonde, Nordic looking....versus Dakota, Eliza and Charlotte-- short, black hair, southern European looking. "

Charity looked rattled. "My sister Charlotte always joked how she was the oddball in the family...This seemed to upset my parents, who were usually easy going people."

Dr. Everett felt he was close to finding a key piece of his puzzle that had eluded him for years. "It is vital that you do not share these suspicions with Dakota. These theories will taint her memory and interfere with our study."

"What study? I thought we were looking for clues how Dakota might be related to this Fenton Anderson character. If you think I'm not going to tell Dakota about the malarkey that you have been spewing today, then you have another thing coming, Dr. Everett. Dakota and I don't keep secrets from each other."

Dr. Everett smiled condescendingly at Morgan. "Everyone has secrets, Morgan, even your beloved cousin. Did you know she has been seeing a psychiatrist for years? Or that those disturbing nightmares from her youth never went away? Now, if you love her as much as you proclaim you do, you will do as I say. I am her only hope for answers."

And with that, Dr. Everett collected his notes into his briefcase, and departed without saying another word. Morgan and her mother were left staring at the table, filled with family photographs and mementos, and wondering who they all were.

TWELVE

Lansing, Michigan
Friday, February 23, 1934
7:25 PM

Trevor Moore had visited many bars in his world travels. From the seediest dives, to the swankiest parlors in Europe, he found them all to have similar ingredients. There were the lonely souls, looking for comfort. There were the revelers, looking for a good time. And there were the talkers, looking for a listening ear. Mix these ingredients with an abundance of alcohol, and it was easy to find a new best friend in a room of strangers. Inhibitions were gone, and tongues wagged freely.

He suspected the bar at the Hotel Kerns was no different. He had learned many of the legislators and area business men liked to throw back some beers and swap tall tales in this establishment. It seemed like the ideal location to make some new friends.

The noise level was already at a high level as Trevor walked into the dark bar. There were clusters of cigar smoking men scattered around the room and some singles lined up at the bar. Trevor figured the barkeep might help him get the lay of the land.

Trevor walked up to the portly man behind the bar, and asked for a bottle of beer. As the man handed Trevor his Budweiser, Trevor pushed a five dollar bill across the counter to cover the twenty-eight cent bottle, and some local information.

"Good Evening, "Trevor ventured.

"It is at that, "said the Barkeep, sweeping away the five dollar bill with one hand, as he polished the bar surface with the other hand.

"Say, I'm new in town...trying to get my bearings...I hear this is a favorite spot for our boys down at the Capitol..."

The barkeep nodded ever so slightly to a large gathering to the right of Trevor. "That's the Legislator's Democratic contingency... and in the other corner, their Republican counterparts. After a few more rounds, the two groups will start to intermingle...and to your far left at the end of the bar by himself, is one of Governor William Comstock's right hand men..."

"Are there any men of industry here tonight?" asked Trevor. "No, I don't see any bigwigs from Oldsmobile or Reo...A few traveling salesmen standing by the piano..."

The Barkeep continued profiling the groups, identifying the leaders and followers, and those with clout at the Capitol. Trevor thanked the man and decided to start working the room. He knew there was a small window of opportunity where people were imbibed enough to be friendly, but not too sloshed that they would forget the whole encounter by the next day.

Trevor walked up to one of the identified leaders, and extended his hand. "Senator, forgive me for interrupting your evening. My name is Trevor Moore. I've been told with good authority that you're the one to talk to if a man wants to accomplish anything at the Capitol."

Trevor knew leaders had fragile egos, which liked being stroked. As predicted, the Senator seemed to puff out his chest more and through back his shoulders. The others seem to quiet some and circle around the leader. "What's on your mind, sir?" asked the Senator.

"I have an engineering design that I plan to produce. I'm looking for the right area in Michigan to build the factory."

"Young man, you have some bravado, trying to start a company in the middle of this Depression. How do you expect to get money to bankroll this project?" With that loud proclamation, the Senator let out a big howl which was then mimicked by the others.

"Actually, sir, I already have some seed money obtained. I was hoping I could get your expertise on what area of Michigan may best be suited for my venture...It would bring some new jobs of course to the area..."

Now Trevor could see he was attracting more attention. With twenty five percent of the population unemployed, obtaining new jobs for ones district would be a feather in the cap of any legislator.

"Mr. Moore, why don't you come join us for a beer and tell us about your venture," invited the Senator.

Trevor sat down at one of the circular tables. "I joined the Army to serve in the Great War—"

"Here's to our Doughboys!" shouted several patrons, raising their glasses.

"After the war, I settled in Italy. My father-in-law owned a factory that produces automobiles that are fueled by natural gas...that is a popular fuel in Italy."

"Not much use for that kind of thing over here. Our cars run on oil, Texas Tea," commented one of the followers.

"You know, there are advantages to natural gas. The engines run cleaner, and oil won't last forever, "said Trevor.

With that comment, a loud roar went around the group. "Boy, I think you've been in Europe too long. We have oil gushers booming in this country. Save your money and start up a grocery store, or better yet, a gas station." The Senator slapped Trevor's back and started to walk away.

Trevor realized he had blown the first round. "Sir, that's not my business plan. I was just giving you some background."

"I'm a busy man. Spit it out." The Senator had run out of beer and run out of patience with Trevor.

"Let me buy a round for everyone, and then I'll get to the point, sir." Trevor walked back to the barkeep, with cash in hand. "This should cover everyone for refills. Do you have any peanuts that you might bring out as well?"

Back at the table, Trevor sat down again, this time pledging to be more succinct. "I have a design that uses methane to power farms, and businesses. But instead of getting the methane from natural gas, it comes from very abundant and common sources....manure, discarded food, sewage, grasses—"

"Oh, that's a wonderful idea. I can see it now, the Dung-mobile!" guffawed one of the followers.

"Methane would be an ideal source of energy for rural farms and homes, where it is difficult to get electricity. It would also be very economical for many businesses in cities. Methane gas has actually been used with success around the world. At the turn of the century, areas in England were using septic tank gas for street lighting. And currently, Germany has some public transport systems using methane gas. "

"Mr. Moore, here in American, we have gasoline in our blood. These stories you tell would make a good chemistry class experiment. But on Main Street, USA, this is not going to fly. It's been interesting talking to you. Now if you would excuse me, I think a New York strip is calling my name in the dining room."

Trevor arose and returned to the safety of the bar. All that he had lost was a round of drinks and a little pride, he reminded himself. He still had confidence in Aberto's design. This was just the first act of the play.

As Trevor was allowing for just a tad of self pity while washing down the remaining peanuts with his beer, a man sitting two stools down spoke. "You're pitching your idea to the wrong group of men, son."

Trevor looked up and saw a middle aged man, nicely dressed, looking down at his cocktail. "How is that, sir?" he questioned.

The governor's right hand man replied, "Those men were all politicians, who never had to create or build anything in their entire lives. Besides, politicians like the status quo, and shy away from change. Rocking the boat could land them out of power."

"Good points," conceded Trevor.

"These men have such a limited field of vision. I suspect none of them have ever left the Midwest, maybe never left Michigan. They're used to plenty of land and resources. I'm from New York City. The amount of refuse that piles up there is massive. Picture that in another generation, and I think having a practical usage for that garage heap sounds like a good plan."

The two men sat in silence for awhile. The man interrupted Trevor's thoughts and said, "You need to talk to a wealthy investor, one who is bored with his money and looking for a new challenge... someone not threatened by new technologies..."

"Do you have any suggestions?" asked Trevor.

The man stood up and moved two stools closer to Trevor for more privacy. "I know just the man...He's been at several of the Governor's functions so I've met him a few times. If you are interested, I bet I could arrange a meeting for you."

"Am I ever. Just point me in the right direction."

"His name is Anderson. Sanford Anderson. Family made their money in timber in the last century. I hear he's looking for new projects to explore, and I suspect yours may be right up his alley. Give me some time to approach him. I'll leave word for you at the hotel's front desk."

Trevor thanked the man and was left holding an empty beer bottle at the bar alone. Trevor wished he could compare notes with Aberto. How he missed their long talks and endless debates on science, politics and life.

Trevor had made three promises to the old man on his death bed. The first promise had been easy. Aberto wanted Trevor to return to America. His father-in-law had had many dealings with Mussolini and felt Italy was becoming an unsafe place, particularly for an American. Without Pia and Aberto, Italy was a lonely place for him, and he longed to return to the states.

The second promise had been to make their invention come alive. Aberto had dreamed of seeing their work take fruition but had died before this happened. Trevor was determined to make the old man proud.

The third promise would be the difficult, perhaps impossible one to keep. Aberto did not want Trevor to grow old alone, and insisted Trevor find a new family. The thought of moving on tore at his heart. Trevor had never looked at another woman since Pia died...not until he met Grace Dunning. Something about her intrigued him. He sensed the same strength and intelligence that had attracted him to Pia.

The barkeep walked over to Trevor and placed a cold Budweiser in front of him. "This one's on the house."

Trevor looked at the bottle for awhile, and then raised it up in a silent toast. A tear welled in his eye. I will love you forever, Pia, he thought. But it's time to start working on promise number three.

THIRTEEN

Lansing, Michigan
Tuesday, October 5, 2010
6:15 PM

Dakota took a deep breath and flopped into her desk chair. It had been a long day, and judging from the number of messages and test results needing review on her Electronic Medical Record, it was going to be a long night as well. She packed up her lap top and decided to finish the day working from home.

Her staff had already left, so she turned the lights off as she walked down the hallway of her medical office. Approaching the waiting room, she could see a man through the glass entry door, standing with a box of pizza. Dakota opened the door and said, "I think you have the wrong office. I bet you're looking for the Web design company across the lobby. They live on pizza day and night over there."

The man smiled and said, "Actually, I'm looking for you, Dr. Graham. I was hoping you'd give me a few moments of your time, in exchange for my feeding a hungry and tired doctor."

Dakota focused on his face, and realized the man was Joel Anderson, her benefactor's son. She momentarily hesitated, then said "Who could turn down De Luca's pizza...Come on in. The break room is over here. "

She walked back into the office and flipped the lights on again. The break room was actually a small alcove with a dorm size refrigerator, microwave and a small table. Joel opened the pizza box while Dakota collected some cold pop bottles and paper plates.

Dakota sat down, and waited for Joel to speak. "I'm sure that I'm the last person you expected to see at your doorway," he said.

"I have to admit that I didn't expect the CEO of a corporation to be moonlighting as a delivery man, even for pizza as good as De Luca's..."

"I guess I'm surprised as well...I thought maybe we could help each other figure out a puzzle."

"I assume you're referring to the puzzle of why your father left a million dollar inheritance to some unknown woman?"

"I loved my father very much, but in many ways, he was an enigma to me. I'm just trying to understand him better."

"No one is more at a loss than I about the events that have transpired. I'd never heard of your father before I received the notification about the will. So I'm afraid that I'm not going to be much help to you."

"I can tell you that Fenton is not your father," Joel said evenly, watching her face for a reaction.

Dakota let out a loud laugh. "Unless your father was on an archeology dig in South Dakota in 1977, he's not my father. But I can understand why that thought would go through your mind."

Joel's face turned a little red, but her laughter seemed to have broken the tension in the room. "And I suspect that explains the origin of your name, "he said with a smile.

"Any guesses where my brother Niles was conceived? What can I say? My parents were free spirits...But how did you come to that paternity conclusion?"

"Well, my mother, who is anything but a free spirit, took your used water bottle from the law office, and had your saliva tested for DNA."

"Wow..." She wasn't sure how to respond to that.

Joel looked guiltily down at his pizza. For once, a part of him had been pleased with his mother's underhanded dealings, as he too had suspected Dakota might have been his half sister. "Despite her obvious wealth, it really sticks in her craw that you have inherited over a million dollars from my father's estate. Maybe she fears you and Dad were lovers..." Joel peered up at her face for her reaction. All he saw was a blank look. "Or maybe she's still the little girl, passed around foster homes, who

There was a prolonged silence as Joel waited for her response. Dakota's mind wandered to the deep emotions the name Fenton Anderson conjured in her mind. She considered sharing this with Joel. He seemed so down to earth. But Dakota's suspicious side reminded her that she knew little about this man. His congeniality may be a ploy with his mother, a kind of good cop/bad cop strategy. Keep your cards close to your vest, she said to herself. That had always been her motto and had served her well so far.

She decided to take the lead and turn this interrogation around. "What do you know about the engineering drawings and the room key for the Hotel Kerns?"

Joel noted Dakota had not reconfirmed her earlier statement of not knowing his father, but let it pass. "I'm also very curious about this peculiar collection of items in his safety deposit box. Actually, that's a good lead in to a favor I'd like to ask. I was hoping you would allow me to accompany you when you open my father's safety deposit box."

"You're very direct, Mr. Anderson. You don't beat around the bush."

"It's Joel, and I've never liked playing games, Dr. Graham."

"It's Dakota, and I'd actually be happy to have someone go with me to examine the box's contents. Maybe together we can shed some light on this puzzle, as you call it."

They finished their pizza with light conversation, cleaned up their mess, and Dakota closed up the office for the second time. The pair exited the building, and Joel waved good bye as he climbed into his Chevy Avalanche truck and drove away.

Dakota unlocked her car door and was about to slide in when she was startled by a man's voice. "I thought you were working late tonight."

Dakota almost jumped out of her skin, and turned around to see Alex standing behind her. "Oh my God. You shouldn't sneak up on a woman like that in a dark parking lot. You almost gave me a heart attack, "she said.

"Who was the dude in the truck?" he asked, ignoring her reprimand.

"That was Joel Anderson, the son of the man who left me the inheritance."

"So you have time to eat pizza with a multimillionaire, but when I offered to bring you some subs for dinner, you were too busy to eat?"

"Joel showed up, unannounced, with pizza. And what's going on with you tonight? Are you spying on me?" Dakota demanded.

"Ever since you found out that you're rich, you haven't given me the time of day... You keep pushing me away... I know we could have something between us, if you would just give me a chance to prove it to you... I won't be a struggling artist forever. Things are in the works, and my fortunes will be turning around soon."

Alex reached over to Dakota and brusquely pulled her up against his chest. He tipped her head back, and said, "I want you to be mine, Dakota," and roughly kissed her on the mouth. His passion, fueled by anger, caught her by surprise. But as she gathered her wits, she pushed him away with all her strength.

"Get off me!" Dakota yelled at him. "I don't respond to macho moves, and I certainly don't have to justify my actions to you. Goodnight, Alex."

Dakota turned to open her car door, as Alex grabbed her wrist. "Wait, Dakota. Don't leave angry. It's just that I've been under so much pressure lately... I lost everything that I had built... my career, my family, my reputation...When I met you, I saw hope for a new beginning. And I think I've landed an investor to help bankroll restarting my business. The green eyed monster just got the best of me tonight."

"I need to go home now, Alex. Please let go of my wrist."

Alex released her wrist, and Dakota slid quickly into her car. She drove out of the lot, without any further conversation between them. Alex swore out loud and kicked the ground as he watched her drive down the street. He yelled into the night sky, "What the hell is wrong with me? Why can't I get my act together anymore?"

Unbeknown to either Alex or Dakota, the occupant of a Hummer parked in the adjacent lot was enjoying the show. Thank goodness for digital cameras, he thought. He had taken plenty of photographs to document tonight's drama well. He smiled, and said under his breath, "Things are going very well...very well indeed."

FOURTEEN

Lansing, Michigan
Saturday, March 31, 1934
2:30 PM

S anford Anderson leaned back in his desk chair and lit his King
Edward cigar. "Very interesting design, Mr. Moore. You have captured my attention."

Trevor had been surprised how quickly the Governor's attaché had
contacted him after their chance encounter at the Hotel Kern's bar to
arrange a meeting with Mr. Anderson. Trevor carefully replaced the engineering drawings back in their leather pouch.

"I have great faith that this design could provide inexpensive and reliable energy sources for farms, and small businesses. It would be ideally
suited to rural areas where there is not electricity yet. But it's just as apropos for large metropolitan areas such as New York City. Can you imagine
how much refuse and waste is produced by its seven million residents?
What a source of methane!" said Trevor.

"Now you say your father-in-law's factories made natural gas powered automobiles. Why are you not pursuing that avenue?" asked Sanford.

"The American car industry is entrenched with using gasoline for
their vehicles. As long as there is an abundant supply of oil in our fields,
I suspect his automobiles designs wouldn't generate much interest here. "

Sanford continued puffing in silence, looking deep in thought.
Trevor was not a salesman at heart and was not sure how hard to push.

They had just finished over two hours of pouring over the designs. So Trevor decided to remain quiet as well.

After several minutes, Sanford broke the silence. "I've been looking for a new venture to pursue. This design may be just the right fit. We would need to start with a prototype and then figure out a marketing plan... Why don't we talk finances over a brandy...?"

Sanford walked over to his hutch and poured brandy into two snifters. As the men swirled their brandy, they got down to brass tacks.

"How much capital do you bring to the table, Mr. Moore?"

"Please, call me Trevor. I have the intellectual capital in that I own these designs. My father- in-law willed these to me on his death. I also have some seed money, around $100,000."

"That amount of money is far from what you would need to get this design produced and marketed...which is where I would come in... "

Sanford stood up and walked toward family portraits lining the wall of his library. He studied the collection before speaking. "I have a son... Fenton is a fine young man, but a little...lacking in direction. He will be done with college for the summer soon, and I'd like him to work with you on this project. He will act as the liaison between us."

Trevor readjusted himself in his seat. He was beginning to think that involving old man Anderson may have been a mistake. The last thing Trevor wanted was some spoiled rich kid as his partner.

Sensing Trevor's hesitation, Sanford continued, "Of course, you could always attempt to open a machine shop on your own...I doubt the banks would lend you money in our current economic climate... and many of the other wealthy men in the state are tied to the internal combustion engine and may see you as the competition..."

Trevor realized his options were somewhat limited,, and he would have to put up with this Fenton. "I'm sure Fenton and I could work together, sir," said Trevor.

Sanford smiled and extended his hand, saying, "Then I think we have a deal. We've got a lot accomplished today. I will talk with my attorney about drafting partnership papers that will protect both of our interests as we start exploring the feasibility of this design."

As Trevor accepted Sanford's outstretched hand, Augusta Anderson walked into the library. "Excuse me for interrupting, gentlemen. I didn't realize you had company, Sanford. Grace and I just finished our tea, and I was hoping you could give her a ride home," Augusta said.

Trevor looked behind his host's wife to see his Cinderella standing there. Was it fate or simply a coincidence that their paths kept crossing, he wondered.

"Ladies, allow me to introduce my latest business partner. Trevor Moore, I would like you to meet my wife, Augusta, and our dear family friend, Grace Dunning."

Trevor walked over to the pair, and with a charming smile, said, "Pleasure to meet you, Mrs. Anderson. Wonderful to see you again, Miss Dunning."

"You two know each other?" questioned Augusta.

"Mr. Moore is a customer at the bank," said Grace, not wanting to explain her failed meeting at the Kerns Hotel. "Actually, it's a beautiful spring day, and I would enjoy walking home."

"I believe our business is done for the day. I would be honored to walk with you, Miss Dunning," said Trevor.

"My attorney will be in touch, Trevor. In the meantime, you young folks get some of this long overdue sunshine," said Sanford.

Goodbyes were said, and the pair departed the Anderson home. Watching out the window, Augusta had a vague sense of unease as Grace smiled up at Trevor. Fenton would not be pleased at this turn of events, she thought.

Trevor and Grace started their walk down Capitol Avenue toward the boarding house on Hillsdale. They were greeted by the sweet smell of the flowering crab apple trees and the cacophony of song birds. The grip of winter was once again relaxing in Michigan.

"Congratulations on your partnership with Sanford. He's a shrewd business man, but he's also a very honorable and fair man," said Grace. "I would love to hear about your venture...unless it's a secret," she giggled.

Trevor smiled and replied, "I ended up doing all the talking in our first meeting...I'd much rather hear about who is Grace Dunning..."

Grace paused before answering. No one had ever asked her that question before. "I want to be a medical doctor. My dream is to go to The University of Michigan Medical School."

She was amazed that she had just shared such a personal sentiment with a virtual stranger. Now she waited for usual disparaging remarks to follow.

Instead, Trevor replied, "That's quite a goal. Why do you want to become a doctor?"

"When I was a little girl, I told everyone that I wanted to find a vaccine that would have prevented my mother from leaving this earth much too young... But during my science classes at MSC, I also learned that I love asking questions and figuring things out. I'm fascinated by the wonderful machine that is the human body."

"You and I have a lot in common. I spent years with my father-in-law, trying to perfect the design that I proposed to Mr. Anderson today. It didn't matter that others laughed at our efforts...and still do. We loved trying to figure out the puzzle. And we didn't let the discouragement of others dampen our enthusiasm."

The two mile walk seemed to fly by,, and Grace found herself surprised that she was disappointed when they arrived at the boarding house. "Thanks for keeping me company. I enjoyed our conversation," said Grace.

"I would love to get to know you better, Grace. Would I be able to call on your again?"

"I will look forward to that, Trevor."

Grace let herself into the boarding house and wandered into the kitchen. She found Louise Mann working on the evening's meal for the boarders. Louise looked up and saw her serious friend Grace with a Cheshire cat grin. "What has you smiling today, Grace?" asked Louise as she dried her hands on the dish towel and walked over to the kitchen table.

"I've had the most wonderful afternoon, Louise."

Louise pulled out two kitchen chairs, and motioning for Grace to sit down, she said, "Tell me all about it. I've never seen you look so happy before."

FIFTEEN

Ann Arbor, Michigan
Saturday, October 16, 2010
10:05 AM

D akota was having a hard time keeping her teeth from chatter-
ing. She suspected her shaking was partly due to the cool room
temperature of the radiology suite at Souviens, but mostly due to her
escalating anxiety levels. Dressed only in a thin patient gown, Dakota
was lying on a table for a Magnetic Resonance Imaging test, while Dr.
Everett placed an IV catheter in her arm.

"Would you explain how this test will be different than the brain
MRI that I had before?" asked Dakota.

"Your previous MRI simply showed the anatomy of your brain. This
technology, called a Functional MRI, determines which parts of your
brain are actively working on the thought or activity at hand. "

"That sounds like something out of a science fiction novel...Can you
read my mind with this monster?" Dakota asked as her exam table began
to move her into what seemed like the mouth of the beast.

"There's more truth to that question than you may think. Several
companies are now using this technology to augment or replace the
polygraph test. The traditional polygraph test looks for changes in perspiration, respiratory rate, blood pressure and heart rate to determine
truthfulness. But the reliability of polygraphs has long been debated.
On the other hand, the fMRI uses the premise that different parts of

the brain appear to be involved in lying versus telling the truth. By measuring changes in blood flow to these areas in the brain, the fMRI can become a high tech lie detector," explained Dr. Everett.

Dakota felt anger replacing anxiety. "We need to stop this test right now. After all these years of torment, I'm not about to be labeled a malingerer or hypochondriac!"

"I can assure you that I believe you, but what kind of a scientist would I be if I did not provide some validation data on my subject. Now stop squirming. We have a lot of work ahead of us today, "commanded Dr. Everett.

As a scientist, Dakota understood his position. But this research was more than an academic pursuit for her. This was deeply personal.

Dr. Everett exited the room, with one final admonition to lie very still. The clanging and thumping noises of the MRI began as they started the test. Dakota could hear Dr. Everett speaking over a microphone, "Now, I would like you to tell me the circumstances of your first memory of the fire..."

The years peeled away to that fateful day in June, 1985. Her voice sounded younger as she began talking. "I was supposed to be with my parents and Niles on their trip to Washington, DC. But my third grade class had their end of school field trip planned for the same week. We were to go hiking at the Ledges in Grand Ledge, a city just west of Lansing. We had learned in school about the 300 million year old rock formations that lined the Grand River and about the Indians lead by Chief Okemos that traveled through the water ways...I pictured myself finding an arrow head or some other treasure to impress my archeologist parents...Long and short of it, I pitched a fit and got to stay home with my grandparents...Otherwise, I would have been killed also...." As she lay in the snug bore of the MRI magnet, she was unable to wipe away the tears that rolled down her face.

In the control room, Dr. Everett watched the fMRI images start to form. This part of the story had been previously verified by Dakota's aunt, and thus these images would make good baselines for comparison with her subsequent stories.

"We were about to start boarding the bus when the principal asked over the intercom for me to come to the office. I was somewhat of a nerd, and all the kids started snickering that I was in trouble with the principal..."

Dakota no longer heard the noise of the MRI coils as the memories immersed her in grief. She had seen her grandparents and school counselor sitting in the principal's office, and had known something big must be up. But she could never actually remember being told her family was gone. Those words never registered in her brain. Her next memory was of crying so hard she felt as if she couldn't breathe.

"My grandparents took me home and tried to console me. I don't think I ate at all that day...just sat rocking back and forth... sobbing. My grandmother held me all night, but I never fell asleep....Finally, sometime the next day, I collapsed on the couch in utter exhaustion and fell asleep."

Dr. Everett could feel the excitement growing in him. Tonight he would pour over Dakota's brain images produced during different parts of her interview. The areas of the brain with the greatest neural activities would be highlighted in color. Would the memories that he believed came from Dakota's ancestor map differently in her brain compared to her every day memories? Would this research lead to vindication in the eyes of his peers who have laughed behind his back, as well as to his face, over all these years?

Dakota's voice brought Dr. Everett back from his thoughts. "My Grandmother later told me that I was not asleep much more than fifteen to twenty minutes, when I began screaming about a fire. My grandparents rushed over to the couch, reassuring me that I was only having a nightmare. Still, I cried that my hand really hurt from being burned, and then I ran to the sink to run water over it...The searing pain lasted for several minutes, despite being fully awake..."

Dr. Everett asked, "How was your hand burned?"

"The dream was very short that night, but had very intense and sharp images...I was standing in a road, looking up at a building engulfed by flames, when some type of burning debris landed on my gloved hand. Then my coat sleeve cuff started smoking." Dakota's heart was pounding very quickly as she remembered the many nights over the year she had awaken to running toward the sink in order to douse the flames.

"How did these episodes of remembering the fire progress?" coaxed Dr. Everett.

"The next installment occurred the night after the memorial service for my parents and brother, several weeks later. The fiery car accident had essentially cremated my family, so my grandparents had their remains spread over one of their favorite mountains out West. But their many friends, colleagues, and students gathered at the Michigan State Chapel to memorialize them with poems, antidotes, and songs...."

Dakota remember that the memorial service had actually been a balm to her wounds, knowing how many others were missing her family as well. She always thought it was odd how the memories of the service had faded in details and clarity over the years, yet her memories of the dreams remained so sharp and precise. When Dakota had shared this observation with Dr. Everett earlier, he had thought this had significance to their research.

"I fell asleep easily that night, but early in the morning, the nightmare began again..."

She knew she was shaking, no matter how hard she tried to lie still.

"Describe what you see," directed Dr. Everett.

"There were people trapped in the burning building... I could hear their desperate screams and pleas for help...I wanted to help, but I couldn't get to him...them...I was being held back...Oh God, I have to get to him!"

Dakota was crying, choking on nasal secretions running down the back of her throat. "I'm watching people climbing down ladders and jumping into nets...I don't see him yet...where is he?" she pleaded.

"Who are you looking for?"asked Dr. Everett.

"I don't know! I've never known who he is... I need to get out of here...Get me out of this MRI!" she screamed.

"Dr. Graham, take some slow, deep breaths. Let your mind empty, and relax your muscles...Close your eyes..."

Dakota tried to will her mind to shut off the images, but to no avail. Dr Everett's voice came over the speaker, with a gentler tone than normal. "Dakota, I know this is tough for you. Let's move on from describing the memories to filling me in on your family's reactions to all of this."

Dakota tried to steady her voice, and said, "At first, my dreams were chalked up to the stress and trauma of losing my family. Others postulated that the fire I was seeing was some kind of symbolism of the fire that consumed my family...That was preposterous as I knew nothing of the accident details until I was much older...Lots of well meaning professionals tried to help, but I got tired of being under a microscope.... It became easier to deal with the dreams myself and to pretend that the dreams had subsided."

Dakota thought of all the deceit and lies that had been required to cover this up from her grandparents, Morgan, ex-boyfriends...The cover-ups became as stressful as the dreams themselves.

She continued, "I did notice the dreams seemed to occur more frequently during times of stress...And then when I learned of my inheritance from Fenton Anderson, the sights, smells, and sounds began occurring during my waking hours, increasing my stress exponentially."

Dr. Everett said, "Now that you've calmed down, I want to get back to the actual memories of the fire. I want you to imagine that the memories are a mural that you need to describe with as much color, texture, and details as possible to allow me to capture what you are experiencing..."

They spent the next forty-five minutes imaging Dakota's brain as she tried to be as precise as possible with her narration. Finally, she said firmly, "I am totally spent. We need to stop for the day. Either turn off this beast, or I am crawling out of the MRI."

Dr. Everett knew there was no point in arguing, and he did not want to push his luck. Within several minutes, Dakota had her IV out and was heading for the dressing rooms.

"I will meet you in my laboratory area," said Dr. Everett.

Dakota showered and changed back in to street clothes, feeling more composed and in control. She left the radiology suite, moved into the hallway and climbed the three flights of stairs to his laboratory area. It was Saturday and the normally bustling hallways of Souviens were deserted. She opened the door to his laboratory area. There was a small front office area, with the expected office equipment. She proceeded to open the inner door marked "Authorized Personnel Only", and moved into his animal lab. There were numerous cages containing white mice lining the walls. She understood the reasoning behind animal research, but the ethics left her uncomfortable, nonetheless.

She focused instead on Dr. Everett, who was seated at his work station, making notes in his journals. She walked over to his work station, hesitant to interrupt, and sat down silently. After several minutes, she said, "Can you give me any preliminary information from today's work?"

"Dr. Graham, you should know that research takes time. America is such an impatient society."

"Can you at least expand on the theory that you are investigating? You intrigued me with the discussion on epigenetics, but I still don't understand how I fit in."

Dakota could hear the mice moving around in the cages as the prolonged silence from Dr. Everett stretched on. Finally, he said, "I understand your curiosity. But it is not good protocol to discuss the details of a study with you, the test subject. It can contaminate the data."

"This is my life, Dr. Everett. I have been battling these demons since I was eight years old. This is not an experiment to me..."

Dr. Everett looked down as he spoke. "...Let me tell you a story about a young boy. One day, he was ice fishing with his father when the lad fell through a weakened spot in the ice. The boy slipped into the water and couldn't find his way back to the surface. Just when it felt that his lungs were going to explode, his father was able to pull him through an opening in the ice."

Dr. Everett arose, and began walking around the room aimlessly. "Shortly after this near drowning, the little boy started having repeated dreams. These dreams weren't the typical nonsensical bits of memory that are usually forgotten shortly after arising...."

Dakota listened intently, not moving a muscle, staring at his empty chair.

"He saw a man being lead to the gallows, and then hanged, with hundreds of spectators watching. He could hear the noises, and see the details, as clearly as if he were watching a movie scene...And the images didn't fade as the day wore on..."

Dr. Everett closed his eyes and leaned against a table edge. Dakota waited several minutes for him to begin talking again. "The little boy had always been taught to be a man, to be strong... So he kept the dreams to himself.... The dreams became less frequent, but never faded in intensity..."

Dakota wanted to respond, but knew it was best to remain silent.

"The boy grew up and went off to college. Like all freshman, he was required to take humanities classes, which he detested. But he discovered a genealogy class was being offered and this seemed more palatable. This was long before the Internet, and genealogy actually required scholarly research to do..."

Dr. Everett started pacing around the room again, his anxiety palpable. "The student became quite engrossed in researching his genealogy and traced a maternal lineage all the way back to sixteenth century England. He then made a discovery that would change the course of his life forever...Turns out his eleventh great grandfather was executed in the gallows of Tyburn for his convictions..."

Dakota gasped audibly, but Dr. Everett was in another dimension, seemingly oblivious to his surroundings.

"This great grandfather had been under house arrest, when suddenly he was pulled out of his home. He underwent a sham trial, and was hanged that same day in front of his wife and hundreds of townspeople. Nine months later, his wife gave birth to their daughter..."

Dr. Everett continued, "This student completed his education, and eventually became a respected scientist. Yet, he continued to harbor a secret. He was convinced that his dreams were actually memories passed down from his eleventh great-grandmother. But what was the mechanism to transmit memories? DNA is passed from parent to child, but the gene sequences don't change with our memories....And then the scientist learned about epigenetics...Could this be a mechanism allowing memory transmission between generations?"

Dr. Everett walked over to a sink, and picked up some paper towel to mop his brow that was damp with perspiration. "Of course, one question begets many more questions...Why doesn't everyone experience these past generational memories? Is a severe trauma required to uncover these memories? Could phobias be memories of one's ancestor's frightening experiences? Are animal instincts examples of memories passed to their prodigy? "

Dr. Everett abruptly walked over to his work station and began logging off his computer and collecting his journals. As he packed up his brief case, he said to Dakota, "I'll walk you down to your car. Security frowns on guests being unescorted." With that proclamation, he turned his back on her and began walking out of the lab area.

Dakota had no choice, but to follow. She wanted to talk to him further about what he had just shared with her, but a wall had been put up between them, and she was afraid to breech it.

They walked in silence to the elevator bank in the hallway outside his laboratory and rode to the lobby area. Dakota collected her driver's license that had been left with the security guard, signed off on the guest registry, and exited the building with Dr. Everett.

As she was about to head to her car, Dr. Everett turned to her and said, "The student often wondered if he would ever believe in something as strongly as his ancestor did, if he would be willing to take ridicule and humiliation from his peers, and devote his entire life to his beliefs...But that is exactly how the scientist grew to believe in his research."

Dakota watched Dr. Everett climb into his car, and pull out of the parking lot. It was at that moment she realized that this research was much more than an academic pursuit for Dr. Everett. This research was deeply personal for him as well.

SIXTEEN

G race hummed as she finished getting ready for her work day. For the past few months, she looked forward to her commutes since Trevor had started escorting her to and from the bank. Not even the poisonous quips of her supervisor, Mr. Edgar, could darken her day anymore.

She paused to look at herself in the mirror. She had always dressed neatly and cleanly, but had not spent the college fund on the latest fashion trend of the day. Her simple outfit of a summer wool A-line skirt, ending at mid shin, and short sleeved cotton blouse must seen so pedestrian to Trevor, who was used to the exotic women of Europe.

She shook off the negative thoughts and exited her back door. The splash of color from Louise's hydrangeas brought the smile back to her face. It was too beautiful of a day to let insecurities creep into the picture.

"Buongiorno, Signorina", said Trevor, coming around the drive way. He took her hand and lightly brought it to his lips.

"Good day to you as well, Sir. Have you recovered from our marathon bridge session last night?"

"Next time, the guys aren't playing against the gals. You and Louise are ruthless together as partners," Trevor teased.

They started the walk from the boarding house to the Bank of Lansing. Her arm brushed up against his as they rounded the corner, and she felt a tingling spread across her body.

"So what have you learned from the packet of medical school admissions materials you received this week?" asked Trevor.

Grace silently reviewed the checklist in her brain. She had saved closed to the $800 required for the four year academic program. She had sufficient botany, physics, zoology, psychology and chemistry class work. But she was still lacking in foreign language classes.

"Eight credit hours of Latin and 24 hours combined credit hours of French and German are required. I'll need to take an additional French class this fall at MSC to be eligible for applying for the entering medical school class in the fall of 1935."

"I know one day that I'll be so proud to say my steady is going to medical school."

Grace blushed. With one simple sentence, Trevor had expressed both the depth of his feelings for her, as well as his confidence in her abilities. Trevor was the first man that she had ever met who was neither threatened by her determination, nor condescending of her goals.

Would it be possible to have both a family and a profession, she mused. She had never allowed herself this dream before. Yet at that moment, her life seemed to stretch out before her, and all things seemed possible.

SEVENTEEN

Lansing, Michigan
Friday, October 22, 2010
12:35 PM

Dakota's crossed leg swung nervously under the table. She was having second thoughts since agreeing to meet Alex for lunch at the Grand Traverse Pie Company. Ever since his surprise appearance in the parking lot, she had tried to avoid his phone calls or make up excuses for being busy.

Alex came breezing into the restaurant with his typical rumpled hair and day old scruff on his face. She watched most of the female eyes follow him across the room to her table.

"It's great to see you, Dakota," he said, as he kissed her cheek and slid into the window booth seat across from her.

Dakota smiled, despite herself. His charm was always contagious.

"I'm really sorry for being a jerk the other night...Can we just start over again? Hi, my name is Alex," he said as he reached out to shake her hand.

He continued to hold her hand, with his eyes locked on hers in a soulful gaze. Dakota gently pulled her hand back to her side, and said evenly, "Alex, I'm just going to be straight with you. I have enjoyed your company and friendship...but I' don't see this relationship leading any place other than that."

Alex's face developed a hard edge that she had not seen before. "Alright...I guess I'm not the first guy to be pushed aside when a bigger fish comes along."

She felt anger rising, but tried to keep her voice calm. "This has nothing to do with Joel Anderson."

There was a pause that seemed to last forever. Finally, Alex said, "Sooo...friend...I'm in a bit of a jam. I told you about the investor that I have lined up for my comeback project. He is a little gun-shy and wants to see some capital put up on my end...Would Lansing's newest millionaire be interested in making an investment in her community?"

Dakota was stunned at this turn of events. "I look at this inheritance as found money. It's not mine. Once I figure out the reason I was included in the will, I plan to donate the money to charity."

"Then can you help me out with a short term loan? This may be my only opportunity to right the injustice that was done to me. I need five thousand dollars to apply for various licensing fees and legal requirements...Or was all that talk of being friends just that...talk."

Dakota's face burned. She knew that she should walk away. Instead, she pulled out her check book. "This is a onetime loan...I applaud your efforts at historic preservation and Brownfield redevelopment... But my finances are tight too..."

"That is somewhat laughable, given a million dollar inheritance you are throwing away."

Dakota tore the check off and handed it to Alex, and said, "I've an appointment. Good luck with your project."

The two arose from the table, and Alex slipped his arm around her waist. "We could've been a dynamo couple, Dak." He bent down, kissed her tenderly on the lips, and walked away.

Dakota pushed the unpleasant encounter out of her mind and left the restaurant for the short walk to Comerica Bank. The letter from Mr. Russell's office, verifying her ownership of the safety deposit box contents, was tucked safely in her purse.

Joel Anderson had agreed to meet her outside the bank. Despite her being early, she could see him already waiting outside the bank door. She had always admired the old Bank of Lansing building. She loved the carvings around the arched doorway entrance, seeing something different each time she visited.

Joel caught her eye and smiled as she approached. "Good afternoon," he said.

Dakota returned the smile, relieved to have a companion on this journey. "Are you ready?"

Joel chuckled. "I'm feeling a mixture of curiosity and trepidation... How about you?"

"Ditto..."

As they entered the bank lobby, her eyes were drawn to two large iron chandeliers hanging from the vaulted ceiling. The walls were adorned with decorative tiles and sculpted figures. The ambiance added to the mystery awaiting them in the safety deposit box.

Dakota had taken care of the paper work and administrative duties a few days prior so as not to waste time today. She soon found herself sitting elbow to elbow with Joel in a small viewing room. The safety deposit box lay in front of them on a table. Somehow she knew this journey would change her life forever.

Reaching into his briefcase, he said, "I've come prepared," as he spread some collector's supplies out on the table.

He handed her some cloth gloves. They donned their protective gear, took a deep breath and opened the box. The first thing that caught Dakota's eye was a silver antique box. It reminded her of an elegant cigarette case. She lifted the thin container and examined the etchings. There was an ornate filigree design, but she could not find any identifying information.

With shaking hands, she opened the clasp to the lid. "Is this real?" Dakota asked, as she gazed at a $10,000 bill.

Joel let out his breath that he realized he had been holding. "The Treasury at one time printed several large denomination bills. There were $500, $1000, $5000, and $10,000 bills in circulation. There were even $100,000 bills, but these were only used for transactions between banks... If Dad's numismatist is correct, this bill is one of only a few hundred of the 1934 $10,000 series that remain to this day."

Using tongs, he methodically lifted the bill out of its container, and placed it on a special lint free paper spread in front of them. "Salmon

P. Chase," he said, nodding at the portrait on the bill. "An interesting character...Senator, Treasury Secretary under President Lincoln, Chief Justice of the Supreme Court...even has the current Chase bank named after him..."

"How do you know these things?" Dakota asked.

"History buff...But as Dad says, interesting hobby, but can't make a living out of it..." he said, somewhat wistfully.

Joel continued to lift out eight more $10,000 bills, two $1000 bills and a $500 bill. "These bills are in unbelievably good condition. Any folding or staining brings the value of the bill down dramatically. These bills look like they went straight from the Mint to this box."

After the bills were carefully replaced into the silver container, Dakota lifted out the next item. It was a manila envelope containing two old photographs. She shook the contents onto the lint free paper. The first photo appeared to be of a formal ball, with guests lined up for a large group photo. The second photo was of a couple, dressed in formal attire.

"Oh my God...that's dad as a young man, with a woman who looks like your twin, Dakota!"

Dakota had the same initial thought. She turned the photo over, and in a flowery cursive script were the words "Fenton and Grace, J-Hop Dance, 1934". A chill went up her spine. The mysterious Grace was a dead ringer for Dakota.

"You looked like you've seen a ghost...Do you need to take a break?" Joel asked.

"I feel as if I'm entering the looking-glass...and don't know which way is up anymore...Let's keep going..."

Joel took the lead, lifting out a second manila envelope, and emptying its content onto the examining paper. He studied a typical hotel key from the early part of the 20th century. It consisted of a small silver skeleton key, attached to a red leather fob, imprinted with the words "Hotel Kerns, Lansing, Mich. Room 402" It also advised if the key were found, to drop it in any mail box and postage was guaranteed.

"Why in the world would my father pass on to you a key to a hotel destroyed by fire seventy-six years ago?" asked Joel. He interpreted Grace's silence as unease. "Are you sure you are alright?"

"This is like a treasure chest hunt," she tried to say lightly. "Look at this beautiful leather satchel," she said, pulling the next item out of the safety deposit box. She opened the flap and retrieved the stack of papers inside. The papers were discolored and stiff, and she gingerly unfolded the first several documents.

"These appear to be engineering drawings...The title says Methane Powered Engine for Domestic and Industrial Electricity and Heat Production...Dated 1933...What do you make of these?" asked Dakota.

Joel studied the drawings before speaking. "This is fascinating... This appears to be a well thought out design plan for using bio waste materials...manure, food wastes, et cetera...to produce energy. "

"But that is cutting edge technology...You can't pick up a newspaper or listen to the news these days without hearing about the need for alternative energy sources...Yet these drawings were dated seventy-seven years ago," exclaimed Dakota

"Anderson Research Center is putting a lot of monetary and intellectual capital into the area of alternative energy sources...Yet a lot of people don't realize that alternative energy sources are not new. History tells us that methane gas from animal wastes was used as far back as tenth century BC to heat baths in Assyria. Long before the Prius, there were electric cars and taxis on American roads in the late 1800's. In fact, at the turn of the last century, a third of the cars on the road were electric. There were also natural gas vehicles on the road in the 1930's."

"So how did we get into the predicament we're in today with our dependence on foreign oil?" Dakota asked.

"Many reasons, but I suspect a major cause was the discovery of abundant and relatively cheap oil reserves in the United States. Combine that with the mass production of the internal combustion engine, alternative technologies were pushed to the wayside. It wasn't until the oil embargo of the 1970's that Americans started a conversation on alternative fuels...But by then, our industrial systems and economy were so entwined with oil that there has been much resistance to change."

"I wonder why your father, with his interest in alternative energy sources, never shared these drawings with you," Dakota mused.

"I was wondering the same thing. I wish he were still here to ask him these questions."

Dakota realized that this must be emotional for Joel too. He was still grieving the loss of his father, and now all these unanswered questions were being thrown at him. Without thinking, she reached over and laid her gloved hand on his arm. He leaned his body towards her and nudged his shoulder to hers gently.

"Thanks..." he said softly. The pair sat in silence for a while, seemingly studying the drawings, but both feeling a connection growing between each other.

Dakota broke the silence when she reached for the next item in the safety deposit box. It appeared to be an official looking, typed report. "Look at this...The cover sheet reads 'Pierce Private Investigative Service'," said Dakota.

"That was my Uncle Samuel's agency. What was he investigating for dad?"

Dakota started paging through the report. "Looks like your father hired him to track down Grace...Apparently she left Lansing in the spring of 1935, without any word on her final destination."

"Did he find her?" asked Joel.

"These pages show your uncle looking for many decades. Originally, he concentrated on medical school admission records because that had been her lifelong goal." She continued scanning the report. "Says here that a break came in 1965. Your uncle bribed mailmen to look at return addresses on mail delivered to people Grace had known while living in Lansing."

"My Uncle Samuel was always a tower of virtue...His son, my cousin Philip, took over the family business. Philip didn't fall far from the tree either. By the way, Philip was at the reading of the will, if you remember."

Grace laughed. "Well, your uncle's technique paid off. A returned address provided Grace's new married name and location."

She showed Joel the final summary page. "Grace was married to a man named Ned Davis, who died in 1959. Grace had no children of her own, but raised her young stepson Anthony. She worked as an editor of the Woman's Section in the local newspaper in Savannah, Georgia."

"Other than the uncanny resemblance to you, do you have any idea what is the connection between you and Grace?" asked Joel.

"I don't have the foggiest idea," said Dakota.

"Anything left in the safety deposit box?" asked Joel.

"One more document...looks official...an honorable discharge certificate from the army in 1919. This soldier must have served during World War I. Can't quite make out his name...The ink is a little smudged..."

"Here, let me try...Trevor Moore...Name mean anything to you?" asked Joel.

The sensation in her hand answered the question for her. She first felt a warm tingle, and then her skin began to feel the intense heat of hot debris. This is not real, she reminded herself, but sweat beads broke out on her forehead nonetheless.

"Dakota, I think all this is too much for you. Let's call it a day," said Joel, concern clearly evident in his voice.

"Can you replace everything, except for the private investigator report, in the safety deposit box for me? I have to get some air," she said as she made a hasty exit from the cramped room, her right hand uncontrollably shaking.

Ten minutes later, Joel met a more composed Dakota outside the bank. "How do you feel about a road trip in your future?" Dakota asked.

"What do you have in mind?" asked Joel.

"A road trip to Savannah, Georgia to find more clues to this puzzle."

"I'm game."

"My condo is just down Michigan Avenue. Let's say I reheat some pasta, and we go over your uncle's report more closely. And Joel, I'm really sorry for wigging out on you back there," Dakota said.

"Don't sweat it--no pun intended. This drama staged by my father is really quite unsettling for both of us. I keep going back to that hotel key...Just who was the occupant of Room 402 in the Hotel Kerns?"

Dakota looked down to avert Joel's eyes. She now knew the answer to his question, but kept quiet. After all these years, she finally had figured out the name of the elusive man she was searching for in her dreams.

Eighteen

Lansing, Michigan
Sunday, December 9, 1934
3:45 PM

"That is one mighty fine looking Christmas tree," said Trevor as he admired their handiwork.

"Never seen a finer popcorn garland than your creation, "said Grace.

"And I've never seen such artistry as your tinsel application," said Trevor.

The pair broke out in laughter and plopped down on Grace's love seat. She gazed at the spindly three foot fir tree, placed on her small table. The tree's branches were sparse and the top was crooked, but Grace had never seen a more beautiful sight. Her single room apartment had the bare minimum. The room included a small desk, where she had studied for her French class this past semester, and a small chest of drawers for her clothes. Her pride was a large book case, the only remaining furniture piece from her childhood home, stuffed with books and family portraits. Her bed was separated from the room with a decorative room divider. And on the back wall, there was a door connecting to the main house, where she shared a bathroom with an elderly woman boarder.

"Why don't you see what's on the radio, and I'll get us a couple of cold colas, "said Grace.

Her Philco radio next to the love seat had been a college graduation present from the Andersons. She walked out the back entrance and retrieved two bottles that had been chilling in the snow. When she returned, the sounds of orchestra music filled the room.

"Would you do me the honor of a dance, Mademoiselle?" asked Trevor, his arms spread open.

Grace's mind flashed back to the J-Hop dance ten months ago. The few times she had seen Fenton since, he had looked so sheepish. Augusta had told her that he had lost face when he had vomited all over her. But on the positive side, Fenton had cut back on his drinking and was excited about the work he was doing with Trevor. She missed their friendship, but was pleased Fenton was no longer wasting his life.

"I'm no Ginger Rogers, but I'll give it a whirl," she replied.

She walked over to Trevor, and he took her into his arms. The radio announcer introduced the popular song by Harry Warren and Al Dubin. As the melody filled the room, Trevor began singing along...

"Are the stars out tonight? I don't know if it's cloudy or bright... 'Cause I only have eyes for you, dear...The moon may be high...But I can't see a thing in the sky...'Cause I only have eyes for you..."

"I didn't know you had such a beautiful tenor voice," Grace whispered.

"Grace Dunning, I want to spend the rest of my life making you happy," he whispered back in her ear.

"I love you, Trevor Moore," said Grace, as she rested her head on his chest.

They continued dancing with the music, oblivious to problems of the world outside, safe in her room filled with love.

※

Later that night, Fenton found himself driving toward the boarding house. He needed to be close to Grace, even if she were oblivious to his presence. He cringed at the thought of his last late night drive to the boarding house when he had humiliated himself in front of Grace.

However, he was motivated to reinvent himself as a successful business man and respected member of society. He was confident that Grace would eventually see him in a different light.

He had been toeing the line these past months, avoiding excessive alcohol and studying diligently at school; and he was surprised at how much he was enjoying working as his father's liaison to Trevor Moore. Fenton genuinely was excited about the project, and his father could not have been more pleased.

Still, all work and no play could become a bore. So now that finals were over, Fenton had joined Benny and his fraternity brothers at the campus bar for a night of fun. He would have stayed longer, but he and Trevor had a very important out of town business meeting tomorrow. He was sure to garner points with the old man for being home before midnight.

As Fenton rounded the corner to Hillsdale Avenue, he saw a man walking down Grace's driveway and continuing down the sidewalk. The Reo's glancing head light briefly illuminated the face of Trevor Moore. A flood of emotions surged through Fenton--anger, protectiveness, jealousy. Trevor had no business paying such a late night call to the boarding house. Was Trevor there to see the Manns regarding renting a room? Trevor surely did not know Grace, and she certainly would not entertain a man so late at night in her room.

Tomorrow, after their meeting, Fenton would have a man to man talk with Trevor, and lay down the law. Fenton would make it clear, in no uncertain terms....Grace was off limits.

Nineteen

C harity watched her great niece Dakota and her twin grandsons having a wonderful time decorating the Christmas tree in the adjoining room.

"Dakota will be devastated if this turns out to be true," she whispered to her daughter Morgan. "She may view this as losing her family all over again."

"None of this makes any sense to me, Mother. How can you and Aunt Charlotte not be biological sisters?" Morgan whispered back.

Ever since the visit by Dr. Everett, Morgan and her mother had been wrestling with this possibility. They had dug through numerous old family documents. Charlotte's birth and early life seemed well documented in baby books and Bibles. But Charlotte's birth certificate revealed an oddity that Charity had never noticed before. Her sister Charlotte was born about 45 miles away from Lansing in the small town of Pinckney, Michigan. Why would her mother have travelled so far away from home when so close to her due date?

"Would you feel differently about Aunt Charlotte if you are not genetically related?" asked Morgan

"Absolutely not. It is our shared memories, the good times and the bad, which made us a family. It is the Alzheimer's that is stealing my sister away from me, not any dissimilarity of our DNA."

"I did some research on line about this Dr. Everett character. He has some way out there theories on memories...Seems he suspects memories can be passed from parent to prodigy genetically. Do you think he could be using Dakota as some kind of guinea pig for his experiments?" asked Morgan.

The women continued looking at Dakota in the next room, as if seeing her for the first time. If Dr. Everett's claims were true, would this revelation fracture their close knit family? Would the memories of shared vacations, and holidays, as well as memories of shared loss and grieving keep them together as a unit? Or would the tug of an ancestral memory, whatever that would mean, rip them apart?

TWENTY

T revor awoke with a start from loud banging on his hotel room door. "Get a move on it! We are going to be late," yelled Fenton through the closed door.

Trevor jumped out of bed, realizing he had overslept on a very important day. He and Fenton were driving to Jackson to meet with some key investors.

"Hey...Sorry Fenton...Meet you shortly in the cafeteria," Trevor yelled back. Trevor was always punctual. Of all the days to oversleep, he lamented, as he hastily brushed his teeth and washed his face in a wash bowl. Luckily he had bathed and shaved before going to bed. His hair was cut short on the sides, but was long on top. Usually parted on the side, his unruly hair often drooped over his eye. Today, he carefully slicked his hair straight back with oil. After donning his best suit, top coat and fedora, he was ready to meet Fenton.

He descended the three flights of stairs and made his way to the cafeteria where he found Fenton drinking a cup of coffee.

"I guess I'm no longer the irresponsible member of the team," Fenton said.

Trevor was surprised at more than a hint of sarcasm in Fenton's tone. Despite his initial reluctance, Trevor had found Fenton to be a pleasant chap, and a hard worker with good ideas. So Trevor chalked up Fenton's sour mood to having a bad day.

After a quick breakfast roll and coffee, the men exited the Hotel

Kerns, climbed into the Reo parked at the front curb and headed towards US 127 for the 40 mile trip to Jackson. Fenton was unusually quiet while driving, so Trevor's mind drifted to his plans for later in the day. He had planned to wait until Christmas, but he couldn't contain himself any longer. Tonight, he would ask Grace to make him the happiest man on earth.

The white snow covered fields of the Michigan countryside slipped by the Flying Cloud. A series of bright red roadside advertising signs caught Trevor's eye. The first stated, "HE HAD THE RING"... about every 100 feet later, another read... "HE HAD THE FLAT"... "BUT SHE FELT HIS CHIN"..."AND THAT WAS THAT"..."BURMA-SHAVE"...He laughed under his breath. He'd have to remember that well timed advice.

The meeting in Jackson passed uneventfully. The business men and suppliers they met seemed genuinely interested in their venture, and pledged to visit their prototype build in Lansing after the holidays. Trevor and Fenton found themselves back on the road by 4:00 in the afternoon, well ahead of schedule.

"Meeting went well," said Trevor.

"Were you expecting otherwise?" asked Fenton.

"Hey buddy, you've had a chip on your shoulder the whole day. Want to tell me what this is all about?" asked Trevor.

"I'm not your buddy. I'm the liaison to your largest investor. But we do need to come to an understanding about an important issue that has come to my attention when we reach Lansing."

Trevor sat quietly, completely dumbfounded. Where was this attitude coming from? Trevor noted the sky was darkening ominously, reflecting the mood in the Reo. Soon, sleet began falling over the tar and gravel two-lane highway. Trevor wished Fenton would slow down some given the driving conditions, but Trevor knew at this point that advice would be unappreciated.

Trevor was having a hard time keeping his eyes open, thinking that maybe he would take a short nap before getting back to the Kerns. As he started to drift off, Trevor heard Fenton swear loudly, while the Reo started to swerve. Trevor's eyes flew open just in time to see a beautiful eight-point buck jump in front of them and run into the field. But Fenton in the mean time had lost control of the Reo. The men ricocheted between the dashboard and seat as they slid into the drainage ditch next to the road.

Suddenly everything was silent and still. Trevor felt a searing pain in his right shoulder that had taken the brunt of the force. He looked over at Fenton, who was resting against the steering wheel. A trickle of blood was running down Fenton's forehead.

"You okay?" Trevor yelled.

Fenton groaned and slowly leaned back in his seat.

"See if you can push open your door. Mine is jammed, "said Trevor.

Fenton and Trevor crawled out the driver's door and were greeted by a cold blast of air. A front was moving through, and the temperatures were dropping quickly.

"I noticed a farm a few miles back," said Trevor.

The men began silently walking down Highway 127. Trevor doubted there would be any opportunities for hitch hiking. Anyone with common sense would not be out driving in this sleet. They finally caught sight of the farm. Trevor prayed that they would find some hospitality, as the men were not dressed for surviving the elements.

Trevor's fingers felt numb as he knocked on the farm house door. Eventually an older man, with deep set wrinkles from a life under the sun, opened the door.

"We had an accident with our automobile up the road...It's not drivable anymore. Would we be able to impose on you for some shelter tonight until we can get some help in the morning to get back to Lansing?"asked Trevor.

"We'd certainly compensate you for your trouble," added Fenton.

The farmer studied the two men, dressed in their finest clothes, as if he were sizing up a new steer.

"You city boys sure wouldn't survive the night out there...Tell you what...I'm goin' to Lansing early in the morning to deliver eggs and milk to some businesses. You're welcome to ride along. You can bunk in the mud room where my farm hands sleep during pickin' season. Nothing fancy, but it's warm."

"Much obliged," said Trevor and followed the farmer into the mud room. The farmer disappeared into the main house, but returned shortly with a couple of wool blankets, some fresh baked bread, and a pitcher of water for the weary travelers.

"Out house is around the back. We'll be on the road shortly after midnight." With that, the farmer was gone again.

"I'm sorry I got us into this mess..." Fenton mumbled.

"We're safe. We're warm. And we'll have a hell of a story to tell about the eight pointer that got away. Get some sleep, buddy," said Trevor, patting Fenton on the back. Trevor threw his blanket down on one of the old wooden cots and was asleep almost as soon as his head hit the pillow.

Fenton stared at the ceiling. He could hear Trevor's rhythmic breathing, but sleep would not come easily tonight....not with thoughts of telling his dad about the crumpled $870 Reo, or of remembering the childish way he had acted today. Trevor had always treated him as an equal, despite their age difference. Fenton would apologize once back in Lansing. He imaged them laughing about the misunderstanding over a beer. Fenton closed his eyes and finally drifted off to sleep.

Sometime after 2:00 am, Fenton and Trevor found themselves standing in front of the Hotel Kerns in Lansing. They gratefully thanked the farmer for his help, and waived him farewell as he pulled away in his Ford Model A truck to distribute his cargo.

"Trevor, let me buy you a beer...I'd like to talk to you about something," said Fenton.

"I'm going to take a rain check, Fenton. My shoulder is really throbbing. I just want to hit the hay...I'll need to be up in a few hours if I'm going to walk Grace to work—"

"Why are you going to walk Grace to work?" interrupted Fenton.

"A man should walk his sweetheart to work, don't you think?" Trevor smiled, and winked at Fenton. "Good night now." And with that, Trevor disappeared into the hotel.

Whether due to his head injury, lack of sleep, or Trevor's proclamation of a relationship with Grace, Fenton felt his head spinning. He stood looking blankly into the brightly lit lobby, wondering what his next step should be. Fenton had tried to convince himself that he had misinterpreted Trevor's late night visit to Grace's house, but now he knew better. He needed to put a stop to this.

Fenton entered the hotel. He wished he had brought his flask. A little imbibing would help steel his resolve. He was surprised to see people still milling around in the lobby, despite the late hour.

"A lot of activity tonight," commented Fenton to the porter.

"Almost all of our 211 rooms are full tonight, sir," said the porter. "That includes some twenty-seven legislators, back for a special session at the capitol. I'm sure you read in the papers about the votes for Attorney General and Secretary of State needing to be recounted from November's election."

Fenton nodded, without really paying attention. His mind was wondering if the bar was still open.

The porter seemed in a talkative mood. He lowered his voice and leaned toward Fenton, as if in confidence. "Between you and me, sir, there's been plenty of hilarity tonight. The beverages have been flowing freely, if you know what I mean."

Fenton bid the porter good night, and walked over to the bar. The room was empty, but he did spy a pack of Lucky Strikes that had been left on a table. Smoking was another one of his vices that he had given up this year. Grace had warned him several times that smoking was bad for his lungs, and he had to admit that he no longer woke up coughing since quitting. But tonight, a couple of drags seemed in order.

Fenton lit up and sat smoking in the dark room for a few minutes. He then proceeded to the stairwell. He could hear singing from some rowdy businessmen as he made the trek to the fourth floor. He recognized the refrain..."There'll be a hot time in the old town tonight..." He bet they had some hooch, but it was time to deal with the issue at hand.

As he walked towards room 402, Fenton took one last drag on his cigarette, and threw the butt at a large brass spittoon in the hallway. He pounded on Trevor's door with three sharp knocks. When there was no reply, he raised his fist to pound again just as the door opened to Trevor, clad in a night shirt, with rumpled hair.

"Fenton, what in tarnation are you doing here?" demanded a clearly irritated Trevor.

"We need to talk," said Fenton, as he pushed his way past Trevor into his room.

"Listen, I put up with your behavior yesterday, but I've reached my limit—"

"You need to stay away from Grace, "interrupted Fenton. "What?"

"You heard me. She's off limits."

Trevor stood silently for a moment. "Is that what this is all about? Do you have a crush on Grace?"

"I'm in love with her. She's already a part of my family. You need to butt out."

Trevor tried his best to control his temper. "I certainly can understand why you care about Grace. And you'll always have a special place in her heart. But Grace and I are a couple, Fenton. In fact, I plan to ask her to marry me tonight, and –"

"That shows how little you know about her! She doesn't want to get married. She wants to go to medical school next fall."

Trevor took a couple deep breaths and replied, "The two activities aren't mutually exclusive, you know."

Fenton paused for a second. It had never crossed his mind that a married woman could or would go to college. But his contemplation did not last long.

"You're ten years her senior, and you have already been married. You're not right for her. You need to stay away from Grace!" Fenton repeated as he grabbed the collar of Trevor's night shirt.

Trevor pushed Fenton off and turned towards his bed to look for his robe. His room was always chilly, and it looked like this conversation was not ending soon. "Look, if you can't grow up and accept this, then maybe the Andersons aren't the right fit for this project after all."

Fenton was fuming. First he had lost his car. Now, he was losing his girl and his job to this guy. Just who did Trevor think he was anyway?

As he turned to face Fenton, Trevor's hands were busy tying the belt around his robe. Otherwise, Trevor might have had a chance to deflect the strong right hook that Fenton threw at him. The punch landed squarely over Trevor's temple, and he fell back on his bed.

Fenton looked down at the motionless man. Trevor would wake up in the morning with a headache. But the punch did not resolve any of the problems at hand. Fenton would be damned if he'd let Trevor take away the project that both he and his father had invested so much time and money in already.

When Fenton was about to leave the room, he spotted the leather pouch that housed all the engineering designs for their venture. On a spur of the moment decision, Fenton grabbed the pouch, stuck it in his top coat inner pocket and slammed shut the room door behind him.

What more could go wrong, he thought, as he left Trevor's room. He knew his father would be anxiously awaiting an update at breakfast. How was Fenton going to explain this turn of events?

The revelry seemed to have subsided, with the halls and lobby standing quiet and empty on his return trip to the bar. He collapsed into a chair and laid his throbbing head on the table. He closed his eyes for what seemed only a few minutes. When he reopened his eyes, his watch showed that it was now past five a.m. The short nap had cleared Fenton's head. Fenton knew he must return the engineering drawings to Trevor's room, and then return home to face the music.

Walking back toward the lobby, Fenton was met by a strong, pungent odor, triggering a coughing fit. The once empty lobby was still darkened, but now swarms of people in their night clothes were rushing about.

Trevor spotted the previously talkative porter, and yelled, "What's going on?"

The man looked up with terror in his face, and yelled back, "The hotel is on fire, sir! Get out at once!" and disappeared into the fray.

Fenton felt a sudden shutter in his chest, as if his heart had stopped beating. His gut clenched as he remembered his tossed cigarette butt. Could he have missed the spittoon and caused the fire?

"Oh my God...Trevor! " Fenton yelled out loud as he raced to the stairwell. He did not get far. A wall of flames had consumed the stairwell and blocked his way. He could now hear blood curdling screams on the floors above. A woman emerged from the stairwell with her hair and clothes on fire and ran into the lobby. A group of men pulled the curtains off the window and tried to douse her flames.

"Get out of here, man!" yelled a guest who grabbed Fenton by his sleeve and pulled him toward the front door. Fenton's last glimpse of the lobby was of a night clerk, frantically calling all the hotel rooms to make sure the guests were awake. But the ringing phone would be to no avail for the occupant of Room 402. And with that last thought, Fenton left Dante's Inferno behind him.

TWENTY-ONE

R ain was starting to fall over a darkened Interstate 75, just south of Atlanta. Joel Anderson looked over at his sleeping passenger. Dakota had drifted off to sleep about a half an hour prior, after more than fifteen hours of driving on their trip from Lansing to Savannah, Georgia.

This could have been an awkward or monotonous trip. Instead, the hours seemed to fly by. They played musical trivia games, guessing the artists on the forties through nineties decade channels on his XM radio. They stopped to eat at small town diners. Most importantly, they got to know each other better.

Joel had already learned a lot of background information on Dakota since the reading of the will, mostly from his mother. He suspected his uncle, the private investigator, was investigating Dakota. His mother was convinced that Dakota was a con artist, who had swindled money from his father. His mother did not like manipulators, unless, of course, she was the one doing the manipulating.

Case in point was his ill-fated marriage. At the time, his father had been considering a run for the United States Congress. On one hand, his in-laws had helped many people get to Washington over the years, and his mother thought his politically naïve father needed inside connections. On the other hand, his in-laws badly needed an infusion of

Anderson money. Their "old money" had dried up, and their lifestyle was in danger of evaporating. It was a match made in heaven, according to his mother's definition.

Joel had been too young to see the behind the scenes maneuvering, and had been swept up by the staged adoration of his ex-wife and her family. Fenton, blind to the whole plot, had been on the road a great deal during this time period. His father had never forgiven himself for not protecting Joel.

Joel trusted Dakota and believed that she was as baffled as everyone else as to why she was included in the will. This journey to discover the illusive Grace may provide them all with some answers. But the one thing Joel was sure about was how important Dakota had become to him in such a short period of time.

The rain was really coming down hard now, and visibility was nil. Joel thought it would be best to find a hotel for the night.

"Dakota..." he said.

"Hmm?"

"Hey sleepy head, I think we should find a hotel for the night. Driving is pretty bad now."

Dakota opened her eyes to the wipers sloshing across the windshield on high speed, but doing little to help them see more than a car's length ahead.

Dakota felt uneasy that she had fallen asleep. "How long was I sleeping?" she asked.

"Not long," Joel replied.

They started hunting for signs advertising lodging. Dakota spied a possibility, and Joel pulled off the interstate into the parking lot of a typical 1950's style motel. A neon vacancy sign could be seen flashing through the torrential downpour.

The couple darted to the manager's office and rang the buzzer. Eventually, a tired looking middle aged woman opened the door and let them in out of the rain.

"We need two rooms for the night, "said Joel.

" Sorry, can't help you. Only have one room left, with the holiday season and all," the manager explained.

Joel glanced over at Dakota, and the anxious look on her face answered his question.

"Any suggestions on where there may be available rooms?"Joel asked.

"This room will be just fine," said Dakota, sounding more confident than she looked. Dakota ended the discussion by handing the manager her credit card.

Ten minutes later, Joel and Dakota were standing in their home for the night. The previous comfort between them seemed to have dissipated as they surveyed the small room with one double bed.

"I'll stretch out on the floor with the extra blanket," offered Joel.

"Don't be silly. You need your rest. Why don't you get ready for bed first."

They took turns in the bathroom, and then climbed into the bed without any conversation between them. Lying in the dark, they both stared at the ceiling.

Finally, Dakota broke the silence. "I need to tell you a secret."

"What's that?"asked Joel.

"...Sometimes, I do...strange things in the middle of the night," said Dakota.

"Is this where you tell me that you become a vampire at midnight?" teased Joel.

Dakota smiled in the dark. "No, your blood is safe tonight...I sometimes have very vivid dreams that I act out."

"How long has this been happening?"

Dakota then repeated her saga, just as she had done for Dr. Everett. Sometime during the story, Joel had reached over to hold Dakota's hand.

"So you think my father is somehow connected to your dreams?"

"Yes, seeing the name Fenton in the letter from the attorney's office triggered my first experience while awake. I've come to believe that the fire I see is related to the Hotel Kerns. And the occupant of Room 402 is Trevor Moore, the man I'm trying to find in my dreams."

"Thanks for trusting me enough to share this with me," Trevor said.

"I've slept alone since I was eight years old for fear of looking like a lunatic," said Dakota

"Is that why you looked so terrified to share a room with me?" "I was that obvious?" she chuckled.

"Why don't you move over here, and we'll face the fire together tonight, " said Joel, as he opened his arms for her.

Dakota scooted over and laid her head on his shoulder. A few minutes passed, and Joel said softly, "Dakota, I have a secret too...This may sound like the corniest pick-up line ever, but I swear, it's the God's honest truth...We've only known each other for a few months, but I feel like I've known you for a lifetime...Dakota?"

He looked down at Dakota, nestled up in his shoulder. She was already sleeping soundly. He knew that he was falling head over heels for this woman. It both scared and thrilled him at the same time.

Dakota never slept better than she did that night.

TWENTY-TWO

Lansing, Michigan
Tuesday, December 11, 1934
12:05 AM

At midnight, after hours of expectant waiting, Grace finally conceded that Trevor would not be visiting her tonight. She put on her night gown, turned the lights off, and climbed into bed. Tears stung in her eyes, but she told herself to stop being silly. She reasoned that Trevor must have returned late in the evening from his out of town meeting. She would see him in a matter of hours when he walked her to work.

She had been on her own for so long that she was not used to needing and missing someone. She had opened her heart to this man, and now she felt vulnerable. This made her uncomfortable. Things would be better in the morning after a good sleep, she told herself.

But Grace could not settle herself down, and continued to fret, and toss and turn. Her clock chimed as the hours marched by without any sleep. She had an underlying feeling of dread that she could not shake.

Finally, she gave up on sleep. To hell with her reputation, she concluded. She needed to see Trevor now, despite the unusual hour. She splashed water on her face, brushed her teeth and hair, and dressed in a wool suit for work. She pulled on her winter coat, gloves, scarf, hat and boots and was out the door at nearly 5:30 a.m.

She felt assaulted by a blast of arctic wind that hit her squarely in the face and took her breath away for a few seconds. The temperature felt near zero. She covered her face with her scarf to warm the air she was breathing and began the trek to the Hotel Kerns.

Grace walked quickly through the empty streets, feeling an increasing sense of urgency. She could see the State Capitol Building ahead on Capitol Avenue, with its white illuminated dome seeming to stand guard over the sleeping city. She imagined sharing a chuckle with Trevor that her anxiety had propelled her to leave her warm bed to face these brutal elements. But at this point, her only focus was the need to be held in his arms, and assured all was well.

The winter silence was broken by a shrill fire alarm bell, becoming louder as she neared the corner of Michigan and Capitol. Her mind tried to quell the panic rising in her, arguing that many wooden structures downtown were at risk for fire. But deep in her soul, Grace knew Trevor was in trouble.

She rounded the corner and broke out running down Michigan Avenue, towards Grand Avenue. Grace thought of the large hotel, built twenty-five years ago. The exterior façade was brick, but the interior was all Michigan timber. A fire in such a structure would spread very quickly. She only remembered one stairwell. How close was this lifeline to Room 402?

Her lungs ached as she raced towards Grand Avenue. As she turned north, her worst fears were confirmed. The windows of the Hotel Kerns were ablaze with brilliant orange flames that were lapping up the sides of the building. Multiple fire apparatus were positioned around the hotel, with an army of firemen already on the scene.

And then Grace heard noises that would persist in her memory forever—blood curdling screams from the upper floors. She could see people leaning over the window sills, begging for help from the firemen below.

People were running out of the front door of the hotel in their sleep wear and bare feet onto the icy sidewalks. The victims' clothes were charred or even on fire. Many were coughing from smoke inhalation, while others looked in shock. Grace tried to get closer to see if Trevor was among the fleeing crowd, but she was pushed back by the fire fighters.

Firemen were beginning to raise ladders towards the trapped guests. Grace counted four ladders in all. But many of the trapped could not reach the ladders in time. In desperation, some of the guests were jumping to their demise onto the sidewalks below or into the icy river behind the hotel in order to escape the inferno.

Grace swallowed to keep the rising bile down. One of the jumping guests fell onto a fireman who was attempting to rescue the trapped. The pair collapsed in a heap. Grace was about to slip past the police barricades to help, when she was pulled backwards by someone grabbing her coat sleeve.

"Grace, what in the world are you doing here?" demanded Fenton.

"I have to help those injured men!" she yelled back over the loud background noises.

"Look, another fireman is over there, and is helping them now."

Grace looked over her shoulder. The guest had a sheet over him and was being carried away. The fireman was struggling to stand up. Others were yelling at the rescuer to get medical attention, but the fireman refused to leave his duty.

Grace turned back to Fenton, who was continuing to yell at her. "You've no business being here. You're going to get hurt. Let the firemen do their job. I'll walk you home."

"I'm not leaving until I find Trevor! His room was on the upper floor. They're setting up a net now," Grace said resolutely. They turned toward the Kerns to watch a total of eight guests jump into the waiting net.

Fenton did not like the idea of Grace being here one bit. The wind had really whipped up and debris was flying in the air. It would not be long before the whole building collapsed. Besides, she could easily get frost bite standing out in the subzero temperature. He said the first thing that popped into his mind to get her to leave.

"Trevor is not here, Grace."

Hope swelled through her body, and Grace felt giddy. "Oh, thank God! Where is he?"

"...He left town," said Fenton, realizing he hadn't thought this approach through.

"He wouldn't have left without telling me. Where did he go?"asked Grace.

"...The investors we met today were only lukewarm on the project, so he decided to take his idea to a larger market area, such as Chicago." Even as the words came out, Fenton realized he was making a terrible mistake, but once the lie got momentum, he did not know how to stop. "And quite frankly, Lansing was too mundane for his European, cosmopolitan tastes..."

Grace felt like she had been slapped. "I don't believe you." Turning her back on Fenton, she returned toward the hotel.

She could now see a large group of people had escaped onto the roof. The firemen were struggling to get the ladders set for rescuing them. The background noise level was deafening—the crackling of the wood, the shouts of the fireman, the engine noises, the blustering wind, and the desperate screams of the trapped.

Suddenly, to the horror of all the firemen and onlookers, the roof collapsed. The group on the roof was swallowed up by the inferno. Then all at once, the screams seemed to stop.

Grace felt a wave of nausea overtake her, and she bent down to vomit in between body racking sobs. The loss of human life was unbearable. She was lost in her grief and did not notice the sensation at first. A tingling feeling on her hand quickly progressed to a searing pain on her right lower arm. Looking down, burning debris had set her coat cuff on fire. She quickly pulled off her coat and saw the fire had burned through the wool to her skin. She ran over to a fresh pile of snow across the street to cool the burns.

"Miss, they're transporting the wounded to the hospitals. Better get that arm looked at. You don't want to get infection in your burns," said a fireman, as he rushed by her. Despite the roof collapsing, the fire was still raging. The firemen were trying desperately to prevent the fire from spreading to the adjacent Wentworth Hotel.

Grace knew her next stops would be St. Lawrence and Sparrow Hospitals, but not for medical care for herself. Dozens of critically wounded people needed attention first. That would be where her search for Trevor would continue. And if those avenues were not successful, then the makeshift morgue being set up across the street would be her final stop.

Four hours later, the sun had risen, and the firemen were still pouring water over the smoldering ruins of the Hotel Kerns. Ice sickles hung from the firemen's uniforms as hundreds of Lansing residents, gathered in the streets, looked on.

One of the onlookers was Grace, her right arm wrapped in gauze, with her charred coat pulled around her shoulders. She had returned from her tour of local hospitals and the make-shift morgue, with no sign of Trevor. The only thing left was a feeling of total emptiness inside. How could twenty-four hours ago have been the happiest night of her life; and now, standing on the bridge overlooking the Grand River, she could be watching police, in two row boats, dragging the river for bodies?

TWENTY-THREE

Savannah, Georgia
Thursday, December 30, 2010
9:40 AM

After a restful sleep and a large Southern breakfast, Joel pulled up in front of the last known address of Grace Dunning in Savannah, Georgia. It was a charming yellow house with white trim from the early part of the last century. A large semicircular porch covered the front of the house. There was a For Sale by Owner sign on the small front yard.

From the private investigator's report, they had learned that Grace had been born one hundred years ago. Their plan had been to canvass the neighborhood for any long time residents, and then to check city records. Joel walked around the truck and opened the door for Dakota. Hand in hand, the pair walked onto the porch and rang the door bell.

Dakota could hear a dog barking inside, but otherwise, the home seemed empty. As they climbed back down the porch stairs, a male voice hollered from the backyard, "Come around back! I'm doing some gardening."

Joel led the way down a brick pathway and under a grape arbor to a colorful perennial garden. He could see a man in his mid seventies pulling weeds and wiping sweat off his brow. The man stood up and said, "You must be the couple I spoke with on the phone this morning. Let me put my equipment away, and I'll show you the house—"

The man abruptly stopped talking, and the color drained from his face. Dakota feared that he was about to pass out and quickly helped him over to a chaise lounge.

"Are you having chest pain or trouble breathing?" she asked. "Grace?" he asked in a whisper.

"No, my name is Dakota Graham, and this is Joel Anderson. We've come from Lansing, Michigan, and are looking for information on a Grace Dunning...Can I get you some water?"

The color was coming back into the gentleman's face. "It was like seeing a ghost. Young lady, you're the spittin' image of my stepmother when I first met her back in 1939...But I've never heard the name Dunning before...Are you related to Grace?"

"That's the puzzle we're attempting to solve on this journey, "said Joel.

"Where're my manners. Please, come into the house for some ice tea, and we can talk."

Dakota helped the gentleman stand up, and his vigor seemed to be returning. They followed him into the back door, and were greeted by an exuberant Golden Retriever.

"Sparky loves everyone. Get down, girl...This house has always had a Golden since we moved here in 1940...Suspect that will change with the new owners..." the gentleman said wistfully. "My name is Anthony Davis, but everyone calls me Tony...that is, except Grace. She always called me Anthony."

The kitchen had obviously been redone in recent years with new white cabinets and granite counter tops. "Make yourself comfortable in the parlor, "said Tony.

The parlor had bright sunshine streaming in the windows. The original hardwood floor was in immaculate condition. The furniture and accessories looked like they had been professionally decorated.

Tony walked into the parlor, and handed everyone a tall glass of ice tea.

"Your home is beautiful, Tony, "said Dakota as they settled into comfortable chairs.

"Thanks. It was all updated ten years ago when we turned the house into a bed and breakfast...Now the wife wants to move closer to the grandkids, so I'll be leaving the only home I've ever really known soon," said Tony.

"Tony, when my father, Fenton Anderson, died, he left some cryptic messages in his will. He implied some type of relationship between Dakota and Grace. We found a private investigator report tracking Grace to this house. Do you know if my father ever came here to visit?" asked Trevor.

"I read about your father dying in the newspaper. He was quite an entrepreneur and humanitarian, from what I've read. I'm sorry for your loss. But I've never heard his name in connection with Grace before, "said Tony.

"Could we impose on you to tell us about Grace?"asked Dakota.

"It would be my pleasure...She was the most important person in my life while I was growing up, but no one except me is left who knew her... Never hear her name mentioned anymore...Without talking about her, the memories start to fade, you know what I mean?...That's why I still have some old moldy boxes of her belongings out in the garage...They were up in the spare bedroom, but with the B&B, wife made me move them...Wonderful woman, but she hates clutter..."

Grace and Joel looked at each other, both thinking the same thing, that these boxes may be pay dirt.

"But please, pardon my rambling on...My biological mother left when I was just an infant. Never did know anything about her. We were living in Detroit at the time. My father was a newspaper reporter, and Grace was a proof reader. It was love at first sight for my father, but my dad later told me it took several years for him to convince Grace to marry him. "

"Did Grace ever talk about her roots in Lansing?" asked Joel.

"No, in fact I thought she grew up in an orphanage in Detroit. She never talked about the past prior to when she came into our life. I just assumed it had been too painful to remember..."

"So how did you end up in Savannah?" asked Joel.

"My father was offered a better position at the local paper here. So soon after they married, we moved into this house. Except for my years at college and law school, I've lived here ever since."

"Did your father and Grace have any children together?" asked Dakota.

"No, my father had a bad case of mumps after I was born, which I suspect left him infertile. But we were a very close and happy family. I had a wonderful childhood, and as far as Grace and I were concerned, she was my mother and I was her son."

"What was Grace like?" asked Dakota.

"Loving...intelligent...full of life. She always pushed me to reach my potential. She spent many nights helping me with my algebra homework or quizzing me for biology tests. I have no doubt that without her passion for education, I never would have made it into law school.

"It sounds like she was very well educated for a woman of that generation," said Dakota.

"Indeed. The move to Savannah was good for her career as well. She was hired by the paper to work in what used to be called the Women's Section. Eventually, she worked her way up to be the section editor. She steered the section away from its focus on what she called fluff, and included information that woman could use in their everyday life. She took real pride in her work, and was recognized with journalism excellence awards. "

"When did your parents pass away?" asked Dakota.

"My father died suddenly in 1959, from a heart attack. It was a shock to both Grace and me, but we got through the grief together."

"And Grace?" Dakota prodded.

"She died June 16th, 1965...I had just seen her a few days prior at my law school graduation ceremony. She had seemed in good spirits and was dealing with her challenges as much as could be expected."

"Her challenges?" asked Joel.

"Grace had been diagnosed with Insulin Dependent Diabetes. The disease took a toll on her health. Her vision was affected, and she also developed some kidney problems. But I was not prepared for the phone call I received telling me that her aide had found her dead on the kitchen floor."

Tony started pacing around the room, and Dakota was worried that they were drudging up too many painful memories. "Tony, if this is too much for you, we don't have to go any further, "offered Dakota.He did not seem to be listening to Dakota, but rather was in a world of his own. "The coroner ruled that Grace died of an accidental over-dose of insulin...But the rumors were that she took her own life," Tony said.

Dakota sharply inhaled her breath. She was not anticipating this turn of events. "It must have been very difficult in her day to gauge the proper amount of insulin to use. There were no glucometers for patients to monitor their blood sugar. Urine dipsticks were available, but would only give a rough estimate of the blood sugar that occurred earlier in the day," she said.

Tony stopped pacing and looked at Dakota. "Grace's eye sight was such that her aide needed to draw up her insulin syringes. The aide reported that Grace had used several syringes that evening, instead of the usual one."

"Could she simply have been forgetful that day?" asked Trevor.

"You didn't know Grace. She had a mind like a steel trap, "said Tony.

The doorbell interrupted their conversation, and Tony excused himself to answer the door.

"We need to see those moldy boxes," whispered Joel.

"I agree," whispered Dakota back.

Tony came back with prospective buyers in tow. "I'd like to finish our conversation if you folks want to relax a bit while I give a home tour, "said Tony.

"Tony, would we be able to look at those boxes you mentioned while we wait for you?" asked Grace.

Tony looked reluctant to hand over his precious remnants of his stepmother. Dakota's heart was warmed by his protectiveness of Grace.

After a long pause, Tony said, "Normally I wouldn't let strangers paw through her belongings...I've never even looked through her papers out of respect for her privacy...But somehow I feel Grace would want you to learn about her, Dakota...Boxes are labeled, on the shelf in the back of the garage. Help yourselves."

TWENTY-FOUR

Lansing, Michigan
Friday, December 14, 1934
6:30PM

Fenton sat at his father's mahogany desk, staring blankly into the library that had been the project's makeshift headquarters. He remembered as a boy imagining someday conducting business from this spot, with all its associated responsibilities and respect. When his father had offered Fenton use of the library for the project, Fenton had felt so proud of his father's faith in him.

And now, Fenton had destroyed everything...The project was dissolved...Trevor was dead...And the Kerns had been reduced to rubble. Could his carelessness with his cigarette butt have been responsible for the death of thirty-four people and injuring forty-four others?

Fenton had hardly slept, eaten or even moved since leaving Grace the morning of the fire. His father Sanford was too immersed in his own grief to notice Fenton's behavior, and had barely reacted to the lie that Trevor had left town. The fire had killed seven Michigan Legislators, three of which had been very close personal friends of his father.

Four days' worth of the Lansing State Journal lay unread in front of him on the desk. With trembling hands, he picked up one of the copies that included a partial list of the dead and injured. The hotel ledger was destroyed, reported the newspaper, compounding the difficulty in identifying the bodies. Fenton noted that Trevor's name was nowhere to be seen.

He continued surveying the articles, looking for theories on the cause of the fire. Several people had seen Fenton walking the halls late that night...Would he be implicated? Today's paper had a summary of the timeline that had been pieced together from various witnesses. Apparently, there had been a delay of up to forty minutes after smoke was detected before the alarm was called. The employees were looking for the source of the smoke on their own. Investigators postulated that had the alarm been sounded earlier, many more people may have been saved.

As he continued reading, Fenton felt his heart jump in his chest. The article quoted witnesses as saying that the fire had begun in Room 134, on the second floor of the northwest corner of the building. This was quite a distance from the spittoon that he had used. With arms wrapped around him, Fenton started rocking back and forth, sobbing, and thanking God that he was not responsible for the carnage.

His mother Augusta walked into the library, and saw Fenton overwhelmed by emotion. She walked over and put her arms around her son to comfort him. Fenton felt guilty that his emotions were from a selfish sense of relief, but accepted his mother's love hungrily anyway

"I can't believe so many fine people were lost this week, "said Augusta. "Even President Roosevelt wired Governor Comstock to express his sympathies for the victims and their families."

"How's Father doing?" asked Fenton, wiping his face with his handkerchief.

"He's devastated, not doing well at all...We need to support him. Your father likes to act tough, but he loves very deeply," said Augusta. "What can we do to help?"

"Mayor Templeton has announced that tomorrow there'll be memorial services to honor those who died. The Protestant service will be at Plymouth Congregational Church, with a loud speaker at First Presbyterian Church for overflow. And a Catholic service will be at St. Mary's Cathedral. The church bells will toll for two minutes in honor of the victims. The mayor is asking those not at church to observe two minutes of silence. You, your sister and I need to be by your father's side tomorrow for the service."

Fenton leaned his head against his mother, and squeezed his eyes shut. But he knew that the vision of Trevor laying unconscious in his bed, engulfed in flames, could not be shut out of his memory that easily. That memory would haunt Fenton until the day he died, and beyond.

TWENTY-FIVE

Savannah, Georgia
Thursday, December 30, 2010
11:30 AM

Dakota and Joel had found the old moving crates and had carried them out to the patio. For the past hour, they had carefully waded through the memories of Grace's life, reduced to piles of papers and mementos.

There were numerous newspaper articles with the byline of Grace Davis, and commendations for her work as a journalist. There were family photos, vacation souvenirs, and homemade cards from Tony to his mother. All of these added to the tapestry of Grace's life, but offered no insight into the mystery that had prompted their journey to Savannah. None of the items predated her marriage to Ned Davis. It was as if Grace were born at twenty-nine years old..

Dakota stood up to stretch. "Feels like we've reached a dead end," she stated.

"Ye of little faith," said Joel, as he lifted out a large wooden vintage cigar box, similar to those he had seen at his Grandfather Anderson's home.

Inside, there were several old photographs, clearly from the early part of the twentieth century. "Here's a portrait of a man and woman, with the inscription Clara and Adam Dunning, Mother and Father, 1910," said Dakota.

At the bottom of the cigar box were two booklets for funeral services, one for each of Grace's parents. Dakota felt a tug at her heart when she realized Grace had lost her parents at a young age as well.

Joel had already moved on from the photos and was retrieving another item. It was a leather folder that stored stationary supplies, used when letter writing was commonplace.

Joel interrupted Dakota's thoughts and said," Hey, come look at this...We may have something here."

Tucked inside the front cover flap was a letter, postmarked May 15, 1965, from Lansing, Michigan.

"Do you know someone named Louise Mann on Hillsdale Avenue in Lansing?" asked Joel.

Dakota felt butterflies in her stomach. "That's my Great Nana, Charity's and Charlotte's mother."

Dakota and Joel looked at each other. Without words between them, they knew this was the pay dirt.

"Do you want to open it?" asked Joel.

"No...Would you read it out loud?" she said quietly.

The pair walked over to sit on a shady bench, and Joel began reading:

Dear Grace,

I am sorry it has been so long since my last letter. We are all well here. Charlotte is off for the summer after teaching high school chemistry and biology last year. But Eliza, now eight years old, will keep Charlotte busy this summer. Eliza's quite a handful, a bundle of curiosity and energy.

Joel glanced over at Dakota as he read the name of her mother Eliza out loud. Dakota was chewing on her lower lip, eyes on the ground. He continued:

Actually, this letter is not an update on family events. I've been struggling for quite some time now with my conscious. Grace, it's my turn to ask for your forgiveness.

I keep remembering the day you came home to the boarding house, a scared young woman, feeling all alone in the world. You needed a safe harbor to be provided by your best friend. Instead, I took advantage of your vulnerability.

I so wanted a baby. Charles and I had been trying for ten years, and I had all but given up hope. And then, there you were. Trevor had deserted you. You had lost your job. You'd had a falling out with Fenton. And you were an unwed pregnant woman.

My offer to raise Charlotte as my own daughter was selfish. You could have continued living with us at the boarding house, as part of our extended family, and we could have loved you both.

Grace, I have thought and prayed about this decision for years. And I'll only do this with your permission. I want to tell Charlotte the truth. She deserves to know you. And you deserve to hold your baby again.

Joel stopped reading, his voice raw from the dryness in his throat. He opened his arms, and Dakota tumbled into them, shaking despite the Savannah heat.

Dakota's perception of who she was and where she came from had been turned upside down in a matter of minutes. How would Aunt Charity and Morgan feel about her if they were to learn she was not biologically related? So many relationships come and go over the years, but family ties can endure. Would their bond still withstand the test of time?

Joel was concerned this trip may have been a mistake. "Let's go home, Dakota," he said tenderly.

"No, we've come this far. I need to see this through...Is there anything else?" Dakota asked.

"She closed out the letter, anxious to hear Grace's reply and promised to send new family photos soon," said Joel as he replaced the letter in the envelope and tucked it back into the flap.

In the back cover of the folder, there was a stack of yellowed and stiff typing paper. Joel pulled out the bundle and flipped through the pages. A couple of the sheets in the middle of the stack had typing on them.

"Here's another letter... dated June 15th, 1965...That's the day Grace passed away," exclaimed Joel. "Do you want me to continue reading?"

"Please."

My Dearest Louise,

It gives me great sadness to know your heart is heavy. I will be eternally grateful to you and Charles for providing a loving and nurturing family for Charlotte. Under your guidance, she flourished into the exceptional woman she became.

There has never been a day I didn't miss Charlotte. I never stopped loving her. But I made a decision at the time on what was best for her, not for me.

Being a part of her life would be a dream come true for me. But I worry how this will disrupt or reshape her memories of who she is and where she came from. And I also need to think about Anthony. I would not want him to think he was a poor second for the daughter I lost. Ironically, both you and I mothered another woman's biological child, but we loved no less than had we conceived them.

"The letter ends there...Let's see what the next page says..." said Joel, flipping to the second sheet:

I have the most amazing news! The doorbell rang while I was writing this letter. It was Fenton! He tracked me down after all these years.

Now it was Joel's turn to feel apprehension. Dakota instinctively held this hand as he continued reading:

Don't worry. The visit went very well, and I have so much to share with you. But I must tell you the most important thing I learned today. I finally know the truth. Fenton admitted that he lied about Trevor leaving town. In fact, Trevor had planned to ask me to marry him the day he died in the fire. And I have some comfort in learning that Trevor may not have suffered in his death. I can't believe the doorbell is ringing again! Must be Fenton returning for his hat.

The letter ended abruptly again. Dakota and Joel sat on the garden bench for sometime in silence, lost in their own thoughts. Eventually, Tony returned to the perennial garden. The look on their faces answered his question if they had learned anything.

Dakota shared her new discoveries with Tony. Tony cried when reading the declaration of love from Grace towards her son. When it was time to say their goodbyes, Dakota and Tony hugged each other, and promised to keep in touch, now bonded by their own very different memories of Grace.

⸺ ☙☙ ⸺

Later that night, Dakota and Joel found themselves back in the same motel room. In utter exhaustion, they flopped down on the bed, still in their street clothes. Dakota snuggled up against Joel, this time with no awkwardness, and was asleep within minutes. But Joel spent the night rehashing the events of the day. Why would his father have lied about Trevor dying in the fire? What was the cause of the falling out between his father and Grace that contributed to her leaving Lansing? Was there a connection between Fenton's visit and Grace's death later that night? And the most perplexing question was one Joel had kept to himself... Why in the world would Fenton have traveled all the way to Savannah on the same day Fenton had married Joel's mother Candace?

TWENTY-SIX

G race handed Mrs. Green her money, and bid her a good day. The clock showed it was nearing the end of the business day. Her legs were throbbing, but Grace continued to smile and asked the next patron how she could be of help.

Eventually, her supervisor Mr. Edgar closed the front door of the bank, and Grace began the end of the day rituals of closing up her teller's booth. She was lost in concentration when Mr. Edgar's voice interrupted her work. "Grace, Mr. Howard wants to talk to you in his office."

"I'm in the middle of my afternoon tally. Can it wait until I'm finished?" said Grace.

"When the boss calls, you come running. His time is more important than yours," said Mr. Edgar sternly.

Grace wrote down a few notes so she could remember where she had left off. She wondered what could be so important that the bank supervisor needed to speak to her at that moment.

She walked upstairs to his private office, and knocked at his door.

"Come in," Mr. Howard directed.

"You wanted to see me, sir?" asked Grace.

"Yes, come in Grace. Close the door behind you and have a seat."
Her initial irritation at being interrupted was being quickly
replaced by apprehension. She had never been summoned to Mr.
Howard's office before.

Grace pulled up a wooden office chair in front of his massive oak
desk and waited in silence for Mr. Howard to proceed.

Mr. Howard shuffled some papers around on his desk, cleared his
throat, and seemed to be having trouble getting started. Finally, he began, "Grace, when Sanford Anderson first approached me about giving
you a job as a bank teller, I had a lot of reservations. It was not typical
woman's work, and with this Depression, so many family men are out of
work...But I have to admit that you've been one of our best employees..."

"Thank you, sir," Grace filled in the silence.

"It's come to my attention...There's a rumor going around... Grace,
this is very uncomfortable for me to discuss with you, so I'm just going
to be straight forward about it...Grace, we can't have someone... in your
condition...working for the bank. It would damage the reputation we
have in this community."

Grace reflexively placed her hands over her growing abdomen pro-
tectively and said, "Mr. Howard, I haven't missed any of my shifts. The
quality of my work has never suffered. I can continue to do my job...
Please, would you reconsider?"

"I like you, Grace, and I feel for your plight. I'm not totally heartless.
I understand that cad Trevor Moore skipped town on you. But I must
ask that you leave your position at this time. You can collect your last
paycheck at the end of the week."

"Mr. Howard—"

"That will be all, Grace."

"Yes, sir," she said, standing up and returning to the stairwell.

Walking back to her teller's window to collect her personal belongings, Grace noticed no one was making eye contact with her. Everyone,
except Grace, must have known her fate. Apparently, her loose fitting
dresses were no longer camouflaging her secret.

Mr. Edgar walked over to Grace as she was putting on her coat. "I
always knew it was just a matter of time before you'd be fired. Of course,

I thought it would be for incompetency, not for being the town's whore!" he laughed.

"The silver lining to losing my job is that I no longer need to listen to your insults and taunts, Mr. Edgar," said Grace, walking across the bank lobby.

"You better get used to taunts, Grace. That little one you're carrying will get plenty of taunts on the playground when his classmates realize he's an illegitimate bastard!"

Grace turned around, and looked directly at Mr. Edgar," Some of history's most noteworthy men were born to unwed mothers, including Leonardo da Vinci, and Alexander Hamilton." She then continued across the lobby, willing herself to stop listening to his poisonous barbs.

Once outside, the fresh air of the spring day helped to steady her nerves. Although losing her job clearly put her in a precarious position, she felt a sense of relief as well that her secret was being revealed. The shame of lying had haunted her more than the shame of being pregnant. The road ahead would be difficult, but she would face the challenge head on.

But the first step was facing the music with those she loved, but had deceived. She found herself walking toward Sanford Anderson's home, a man who had gone out on a limb to help her find a job.

Ten minutes later, she was knocking on the front door of their large Tudor style home. The door was opened by their housekeeper Luella, a woman who had fussed over Grace since she was a little girl. After receiving a much needed bear hug, Grace was informed that Sanford and Augusta Anderson were visiting out of town. Before Grace could bid Luella goodbye, Fenton strolled into the foyer.

"Grace, wonderful to see you," said Fenton.

"Hello Fenton...Do you have some time to talk this afternoon?" asked Grace.

"For you, anytime," said Fenton. Placing his hand in the small of her back, he guided her towards his office. They settled into two Queen Anne chairs near the picture window. "Would you like some tea?"

"No thanks...Fenton, I have something I need to tell you and your parents. I was fired from my job today..." said Grace, looking down at her lap.

Fenton sighed. He had been wondering when this inevitability would occur. He had been privy to the rumors as well.

"I'm pregnant... with Trevor's baby. I've let your parents down, after they have done so much for me over the years—"

"Hush," interrupted Fenton. "They love you, as do I. We will get through this together. You're a part of our family."

Grace looked up, with tears in her eyes. Fenton reached out for her hands, and brought them to his lips to kiss gently. "Marry me, Grace. Make me the happiest man in the world. I will love you and this baby as if it were my own."

Grace inhaled sharply. Fenton's proposal caught her completely off guard.

"I love you too, Fenton, but I'm not in love with you. It wouldn't be fair to you" she said softly.

"Let me be the judge of that. What do you say, sweetheart?" said Fenton with his patented charming smile.

This was all happening so fast for Grace. It certainly would safeguard her child's future with a loving family. People would think she was crazy for turning down such a generous and loving offer, but something was holding her back. Was it holding out hope that Trevor would return, with some fanciful tale to explain his sudden departure?

Grace heard the doorbell ring and Luella greeting a male guest. Fenton stood up and grabbed a foot stool for Grace. "You rest you feet while I talk with one of Father's associates for a bit. I won't be long." He bent down, kissed her cheek and left the room.

Grace felt overwhelmed. She had been fired and then proposed to in a little over an hour. She owed it to all involved not to decide on the spot, but to at least sleep on this decision.

A glass of water might help clear her head. She walked over to a serving table and poured herself a cool drink. It looked like Fenton was going to be longer than anticipated. She wanted to leave a letter for Sanford and Augusta, so she may as well start working on the composition while Fenton was busy.

She sat down behind Sanford's massive desk, and surveyed the room. She tried to imagine Trevor and Fenton pouring over the engineering drawings, talking with investors, and plotting out their strategies. She remembered how excited Trevor had been when they had purchased property for their factory and were set to begin their prototype production. What had happened to alter all his dreams and plans?

She had spent months of sleepless nights rehashing all the events surrounding the Hotel Kern's fire, but had no answer other than that she had been completely fooled by Trevor...And she refused to accept that answer.

No more ruminating, Grace chastised herself. She had decisions to make, and a new life inside of her to protect. But first, she needed to write the letter. She looked around the desk top for some writing paper, but to no avail. She pulled open the center tray, finding only Sanford's cigars. She reached down to the deep side drawer, and finally found some clean sheets. As she lifted the paper out from the desk drawer, she froze in place. There lay Trevor's precious leather pouch.

With shaking hands, she gingerly touched the pouch, as if it were an apparition. She lifted the pouch to the desk, and slowly opened the flap. She saw Aberto's designs with Trevor's notes scrawled in the margins, and Trevor's silver case where he stored his money. Grace unclasped the case and peeked inside to see his large denomination bills still present.

"I'm sorry, Sweetheart, for the interruption. Let's get back to planning our life together and –" Fenton stopped dead in his tracks as he entered the library. There stood Grace, with Trevor's possessions spread all over the desk.

"What have you done, Fenton?" demanded Grace, with a steely tone.

"I – I don't know what you are talking about, Grace," hedged Fenton, not very convincingly.

"You know damn well what I am talking about. Trevor never would have left town without his precious drawings, the silver case given to him by Pia, or this large sum of money. Now tell me the truth. What have you done!" She was essentially screaming by this point, unable to control her emotions, as she rushed towards Fenton and grabbed his suit jacket.

"What have I done? I'm not the one taken in by a con artist. I'm not the one that has no means of support. I'm not the one who conceived a baby out of wedlock!" The anger rising in him was a good tonic to the guilt that had haunted him since Trevor's death.

Grace stepped back from him as if his words had been a physical blow. "And to think I was considering your marriage proposal. Tell me where Trevor is this very moment. Otherwise I'm going to the police to report stolen property in your desk drawer."

"Now that's laughable. The whole town is already gossiping about your questionable morals. You think people are going to believe your baseless accusations towards a member of one of the most prominent families in this state? I already told you that Trevor left town. I was trying to spare your feelings, but I'll be blunt. He had lost interest in the project, as well as in you. Our company bought the design project outright from him."

Grace knew with complete certainty that Fenton was lying, but could not get past his stonewalling. "I'll take this matter up with your parents on their return."

She started collecting her coat, and gloves to make her retreat. This time it was Fenton's turn to grab her sleeve and say, "As I see it, you don't have too many options, Grace. You can accept my generous proposal of a comfortable life for you and your baby, or you can look forward to a life as an outcast, scraping by for a living. This child deserves better from his mother than that."

"How dare you talk to me about what this child deserves when you obviously had some involvement with his father's disappearance. This child's future is no concern of yours!"

"Someone needs to look out for this baby's welfare, as his mother certainly isn't. This child would be better off in the long run being raised by a stable family like the Anderson's," proclaimed Fenton.

Grace wiggled out of Fenton's grasp. She knew a veiled threat when she heard one. "Leave my baby and me alone, Fenton."

"Marry me, and we'll put all this unpleasantness behind us. Otherwise, I may have to tell the court that this baby is mine. I'm sure I could get custody, given your precarious financial situation and emotional instability." Even as he said the words, he couldn't believe they were coming out of his mouth, but he seemed unable to stop himself.

Grace walked up to Fenton, and slapped him across the face.

Then she ran out of the library, soon followed by a loud slamming of the front door.

Fenton stood in the now silent library, with echoes of the vitriol he had spouted replaying in his head. The memory of Trevor, lying unconscious in the burning hotel room, was eating his soul alive. He knew that there was only one course of action left for him to do. He would first get rip roaring drunk to forget the monster he had become. Then tomorrow, he would apologize to Grace and tell her the truth.

TWENTY-SEVEN

Grand Ledge, Michigan
Friday, February 4, 2011
6:50 PM

Life had been a whirlwind since returning from Savannah. Dakota had been working long days, and trying to catch up at night. On many evenings, Joel had brought his work over to her condominium to share a quick dinner, followed by their dueling laptops going full speed as the television played in the background. It reminded her of being in college and having study dates.

She had only briefly talked to Morgan a few times on the phone since her return, which was unusual for these cousins. Her Grandma Charlotte used to call Dakota and Morgan the "Lucy and Ethel" of the family. The girls were always cooking up some adventure or misadventure together, and had remained tight as they became adults. Dakota felt she could not look Morgan in the eye without telling her the truth about Grandma Charlotte, yet Dakota was too unsure of the ramifications to proceed.

Her work with Dr. Everett had been put on hold since he was out of town for several weeks with work commitments for Souviens. She expected him back tomorrow and was confident of receiving a phone call soon after. Dakota was anxious to share with him her discoveries that Grace was her great grandmother and had witnessed the Hotel Kerns fire.

But tonight was not about work and family concerns and old memories. Tonight was about making new memories. As Dakota drove the ten mile drive to Grand Ledge, she thought about her developing relationship with Joel. Unlike her previous male relationships, her connection to Joel had begun as a mutual support system, and then progressed to a budding friendship. The romance had been put on the back burner, and allowed to simmer slowly over time. If she could read his signals correctly, they both wanted the relationship to come to a full boil soon.

Joel had invited her over for a home cooked meal. While Dakota specialized in canned soups and frozen dinners, Joel fancied himself a chef, and he was putting his reputation on the line tonight.

Dakota had other plans for later on. She had always followed the lead when it came to moving the relationship forward. But this time, she had decided to take the lead, and had packed an overnight bag.

It was dusk as she pulled into his tree lined driveway, going slowly as it was a popular crossing for deer. Joel had personally designed the log cabin style house that was perched on a cliff overlooking the Grand River. Remnants of last summer's vegetable garden could still be seen in the backyard.

Joel had told her to pull into the garage as storm clouds were approaching. Dakota let herself in through the garage door, entering into a wide open kitchen area.

"It smells heavenly in here," she said as she was greeted by smells of her favorite dinner of turkey and dressing.

Joel walked over to her and greeted her with a kiss hello.

"Welcome to Chez Joel. Dinner will be at least another hour. I've got a mug of hot chocolate with your name on it in front of the fire," he said as he took her hand to lead her to the living room.

Joel looked over Dakota's shoulder and saw a back pack on the floor. "Don't tell me you brought work tonight. We both decided we needed a work free zone tonight," he reminded her.

"Believe me, I agree. The bag just has a few things I might need... in case I stay for your infamous scrambled eggs in the morning, "she said, with a slight grin on her face.

Joel turned to face Dakota, put his arms around her neck and smiled, "Are you trying to have your way with me, Madame?"

"Of course. What woman can resist a man who can cook?" she laughed.

"To hell with the turkey. I'm ready for bed now," he said playfully, while nuzzling her neck.

"You're not getting off the hook that easily after boasting of your culinary skills," she whispered back as her mind and body starting going in the same direction as his.

The mood was broken by the sound of the door bell ringing."Ignore it...They'll go away," he said, in between kissing her face and shoulders.

The door bell rang again, and this time was followed by loud, persistent banging on the door.

"I'll get rid of them...Hold that thought," Joel whispered in her ear.

Joel walked through the living room to the front door, totally exasperated by the interruption of their plans. He opened the door, expecting to shoo away a salesperson. Instead, he found his mother Candace and his cousin Philip standing there.

"Mother, this isn't a good time for a visit. I'll give you a call tomorrow and—"

"Joel, you need to make time. This is too important to wait, "she said as she pushed past him and went into the living room. Candace spied Dakota in the living room and said, "Oh...Dr. Graham... I'm glad you are here as well. I think you will be interested in what I have to discuss with my son."

"Okay Mother, you're being rude and obnoxious. I obviously have a dinner date with Dakota tonight. You and Philip need to leave now before I lose my temper."

Candace walked over to the couch, sat down next to Philip, and set her brief case on the coffee table in front of her. "Dr. Graham, why don't you sit down opposite from me with Joel?"

Dakota noticed Joel's anger was rising. Dakota laid her hand on his shoulder, and said, "Let's listen to what you mother has to say. " Joel plopped down on the couch across from his mother, and said, with an edge in his voice, "So what can't wait until tomorrow?" "I'll let Philip present the information."

Philip pulled out a manila envelope from the side pouch of the case, and retrieved his first item.

"Exhibit A," he said, placing several eight by ten glossies on the oak coffee table.

Joel leaned forward to see an array of photos showing a man and a woman, clearly in a passionate embrace, in a darkened parking lot. "What the hell is going on here, Philip?"

"Look closer...dated October fifth, 2010... Notice Dr. Graham with a Mr. Alex Zahn, in her office parking lot, shortly after your truck pulled away," said Philip.

Dakota shot forward, her heart pounding. "You were spying on me, Philip?" she asked incredulously, remembering the unnerving episode with Alex in the parking lot.

As much as Joel hated to see the photos, he was incensed at this invasion of privacy. "If you don't leave immediately, I will physically throw both of you out."

"Son, please, there is more. Let Philip continue. I know this is painful, but I'm only trying to protect you and the company," said Candace.

"It's okay, Joel. I've done nothing wrong, and I'm not worried about what your mother has to say. And this photo is not what it appears to be," Dakota said firmly.

Philip gathered up the first set of photos and laid down another set. "And what do these photos appear to be...dated October twenty-second, 2010...Grand Traverse Pie Company...Dr. Graham with Alex Zahn... shortly before meeting Joel to view the safety deposit box items?"

Joel leaned forward again, and saw more photos of Dakota, dining with the same man, handing him some piece of paper, and then being embraced again. He told himself that her previous relationships were none of his business. But he remembered Dakota telling him that there was no one serious in her life. A sense of uneasiness was growing in his stomach.

"I'm very flattered that you spent so much effort chronicling my movements. But what does this have to do with Joel or Anderson Technologies?" asked Dakota.

"Be patient and you'll see. Next exhibit..." Philip placed a photograph of Dakota's $5000 check written to Alex Zahn on the coffee table.

"Now this is getting creepy. How did you get a copy of my personal check?" Dakota demanded.

"Turns out your boyfriend's ex-wife was willing to share some information for a fee."

"He's not my boyfriend! I ended our platonic friendship because he wanted a different kind of relationship than I did," said Dakota.

"From these pictures, I could see how he could get mixed signals. But to be fair, maybe business partner would be a better term...or maybe partner in crime would be more precise," Candace said, with more than a hint of sarcasm.

"Look, if you have an accusation, then spit it out, Candace. I'm tired of this cat and mouse game you're playing," said Dakota, clearly angry.

"Fine with me. I knew from the start that you had perpetuated a con game in order to get Fenton to include you in his will. Philip now has the proof, "said Candace, without batting an eye.

"Then let's have it, "said Dakota, folding her arms in front of her chest and leaning back in her chair.

"Philip, if you please..."

"Alex Zahn has a reputation for skillful designs and restorations, but unfortunately, for shady business practices as well. A few years back, he lost his business license, and avoided jail time, only due to a legal technicality. He was particularly good at defrauding investors. His favorite tactics were romancing lonely, wealthy women," said Philip.

Dakota thought back at how she had met Alex through an encounter at Scrap Fest. Could this have been more than a chance meeting?

"You have your facts wrong, Philip. His ex-wife, Cynthia, was a paralegal and handled the financial end of their business. She created the financial mess, and hid the situation from Alex," said Dakota.

"Is that what he told you? Of course, an intelligent doctor, such as you, would surely have investigated Zahn before investing $5000 of her own money into his business. You also would have discovered that his ex-wife, a secretary at a legal firm, was fired when she was caught stealing information for Zahn," said Philip.

Dakota had no reply for this. She remembered her reluctance to give Alex a loan, but had been so preoccupied with everything else going on in her life, that she had let her natural skepticism down.

"In fact, the information Cynthia stole was material from Fenton's will," continued Philip.

"Is this true, Mother?" asked Joel.

"Indeed, Son. Alex asked Cynthia to look for women set to inherit large sums of money so he could find his new mark. She offered up Dakota in hopes of winning Zahn back."

Dakota thought back to the reading of the will at the law office. She remembered being escorted to the meeting by a newly hired secretary. Was it part of the scheme that Alex was conveniently waiting for Dakota as she exited the law offices with her new found million dollars? Could she have been so gullible?

"Mother, all you have proven is that Dakota may have been an unwilling victim of a fraud. So now that you've told your story, let's say goodnight," said Joel, rising from his chair.

"Sit down, Joel. We're not done yet," said Candace. "I always thought there was a certain elegance when one con artist was duped by another con artist."

"Next exhibit", stated Philip, placing some type of a receipt and an empty prescription bottle on the table.

Picking up the bottle, Joel read the name on the label out loud. "Mr. F. Anderson...Dad's blood pressure medication...What does this have to do with anything?"

"Look carefully at the prescribing doctor's name, Joel, "said Candace.

Joel's face clouded over, and his mouth felt dry. The label read Dakota Graham, MD, dated September sixteenth, 2003. Joel then picked up the receipt, which appeared to be from a medical office visit for Mr. F. Anderson, with Dr. Graham, on the same day that the prescription was written.

"Dakota, didn't you tell me that you had never met my father before?" asked Joel, carefully controlling the timbre of his voice.

"Of course, Joel. I was as surprised as everyone else when he left me that inheritance," answered Grace.

Joel silently passed over the objects he was holding to Dakota, and closely watched the expression on her face.

Dakota sat staring at her name clearly marked on the bottle and receipt. "Joel, I swear that I don't recall ever meeting your father... This script was written during my first year of residency...As medical students and residents, we see so many patients...I honestly have no memory of any of this...You believe me, don't you?"

Joel had found it hard to trust since his divorce. For some reason he couldn't explain, even to himself, he had very quickly trusted Dakota. He had this sense that he had known her forever. Yet now he sat wondering how well he really knew this woman as he looked at the mounting evidence his mother was presenting.

"I found additional pieces of evidence while cleaning out your father's closets. Dr. Graham, do you make it a habit to invite supposed strangers to important invents in your life?" asked Candace, laying down a program and admission ticket for Dakota's medical school graduation ceremony on the coffee table. "Dr. Graham, you must admit that for an intelligent woman, your poor memory of patients and your poor research on financial investments do seem somewhat suspect, don't you agree?" said Candace.

"Let's just say, for the sake of argument, that I did treat your husband...How does that prove your argument that I'm a con artist?" asked Dakota indignantly.

Candace arose, and pulled a cigarette and lighter out of her pocket. She had quit smoking when her plastic surgeon had warned that all his good work would be for naught if she continued to smoke. She must be really upset, thought Joel.

Candace took a long drag, and blew smoke towards Dakota, who waived it away with her hand. "Dakota, you knew about Fenton's pathological obsession with Grace. You used your uncanny resemblance to Grace to weasel your way into Fenton's heart and estate, convincing him that you are the long lost prodigy of Grace. Joel, did you notice in the video how Fenton said "others" would be surprised to see Dakota included in the will...unlike Dakota, who had already insinuated herself into his life!"

"How dare you say these lies to my face!" said Dakota.

"Grace had lived at Louise Mann's boarding house when she disappeared off the face of the earth with her unborn baby. Grace left behind everything she owned, including photographs. Louise Mann willed her home to her daughter Charlotte, the same woman that raised Dakota. Dakota would have known the story of Grace, Fenton's obsession with her, and the uncanny resemblance she had with Grace. Perfect set up for a con artist. "

"That's where your story falls apart, Candace. Fenton tracked Grace down, and we have Philip's father's report to prove it. And Joel and I read letters from Grace and Louise, verifying that Charlotte was Grace's biological child," said Dakota.

"Perfect lead in...Philip, take it from here, please," said Candace.

"We have archived copies of all our investigatory reports, dating to the start of our firm, on microfilm or CD. There is no record of the report you claim our firm conducted on Grace Dunning. Furthermore, the style and typeset of the report in question was very different than the standard report generated from our firm," said Philip.

Joel was soaking all this in. He had seen numerous reports over the years from his uncle's private investigative firm to support his mother's obsessive snooping. These reports had indeed been of a much different style.

"Fenton never found Grace. He never would have married me if she could have been in his life. Dakota put this bogus private investigative report in the safety deposit box prior to Joel viewing the contents to substantiate her claim she was the long lost relative of Grace. And then she planted letters at an accomplice's home in Savannah, to shore up the deal. Come now, Joel...This Tony lives in the same house where his stepmother died some forty-five years ago...He just happens to keep letters that explain the whole situation... And these letters are so conveniently discovered by you...Even you can't be that naïve," said Candace, waving her cigarette around in the air dramatically.

"And what would I hope to gain from this elaborate farce?" asked Dakota, incensed by this fairy tale.

"Why stop at a million dollars from an old coot who saw in you the love that got away...Why not aim for the son, and his multimillions!"

Joel was lost in his thoughts. He had thought that his father visiting Savannah on the very same day that his parents were married had been rather odd. He also remembered now his father saying in the video recording that he knew how Dakota "liked to figure things out". Dakota had used the very same wording when Joel had asked her why she liked being a doctor.

Joel was startled back to the present when he realized someone was talking to him. "Joel...Joel...You've been really quite. You never answered my question when I asked if you believed this malarkey your mother has been spouting," said Dakota.

Joel wanted to answer, but his mouth wouldn't move. He felt paralyzed by doubt and the old insecurities that women only valued him for his bank account.

"Oh my God...You do believe this garbage, "Dakota whispered, holding back tears with every ounce of her being.

"Of course he does, Dr. Graham. I think I should warn you that I am filing a civil suit against you, on behalf of the estate of Fenton Anderson. And the more I think about it, I suspect the prosecutor may be interested in this case as well," said Candace with a hatred that she did not bother to camouflage.

Dakota stood up, and ran through the kitchen, to the garage, picking up her unused backpack on the way out. Joel sat in silence as he heard her car pull away.

"You had to ruin my happiness, didn't you Mother..."

"Joel, you know everything I do is for the best interest of this family," said Candace, sitting down next to her son and stroking his hair.

"Dakota is an independent woman, with a wonderful career. She doesn't need my money to survive."

"She has lots of student loans to pay, and has a surprising number of medical bills for someone that seems so healthy... And no offense, Son, but you've got to admit that a woman as stunning as Dakota would want to be on the arm of a stud like Alex Zand. Your money would go a long way with helping Zand finance his restoration projects."

"What's wrong with me...I let you do it to me again...I fall for your bull shit and then let you destroy all that's good in my life...

No more, Mother. I don't care what dirt you think you've dug up on Dakota. I know she honestly cared for me. Tomorrow, I'm going to ask her if she can ever forgive me... Now get the Hell out," said Joel.

He walked past the cold mug of hot chocolate, and into his study, slamming the door behind him.

Candace looked Philip directly in the eye, and said steadily, "Time to bring out our fallback plan."

TWENTY-EIGHT

Louise slowly stirred the stew simmering on her Kalamazoo stove. The coal-fired cast iron range had been an anniversary present from Charles last year, and had made cooking for the boarding house residents so much easier. She was engrossed in thought, and was startled to see Grace standing there, her eyes rimmed in red.

"Grace, what's wrong?" asked Louise, leaving the stove to put her arms around Grace.

"Can I help with dinner?" Grace sniffled.

"Everything is all set. Sit down at the table and tell me why your face is all blotchy from crying," commanded Louise. She could not remember ever seeing Grace cry. Even when Trevor had walked out of her life, Grace had kept a stiff upper lip, at least publically.

"I need to ask your forgiveness, Louise. I haven't been up front with you," said Grace, pulling out the kitchen table chair.

Sitting down next to Grace, Louise said, "What's on your mind, honey?" clearly concerned for her friend.

"I'm pregnant, Louise."

"Oh my God...I'd noticed you'd gained some weight, but I never thought...Who's the father?"

"It's Trevor's, of course! How can you even ask me that?"

"I didn't mean to offend you, Grace," said Louise gently.

"And I'm sorry that I snapped at you. It's just...First, the bank manager fired me for being an unwed mother, then less than an hour later, Fenton proposed to me."

"That's wonderful! That solves all your problems," said Louise, hugging her friend.

"You don't understand. I can't marry Fenton. He had something to do with Trevor's disappearance," said Grace.

Louise sighed, and released Grace from her embrace. "Grace, you have to move on, and admit that Trevor was a scoundrel. He led you on and left you in a terrible predicament. You must stop making excuses for Trevor, and thank your lucky stars for Fenton!"

"I found Trevor's belongings in Fenton's desk, including all his money, his engineering drawings, and a gift that his deceased wife had given him. Trevor never would have left town without those possessions. I don't care what anyone says. He wouldn't have left me either. Something happened to Trevor, and Fenton knows about it. I can see the guilt written all over his face," proclaimed Grace, never more confident of anything in her life.

"Did you confront Fenton with your suspicions?" asked Louise.

"Yes, and he became very agitated, and even threatened to take my baby away from me."

"Do you really think he would try to do something like that?" Louise asked incredulously.

"I'd been really proud of Fenton when he was working with Trevor... Trevor had said Fenton was hard working and reliable and no longer drinking alcohol in excess...But since the fire...I hear he's skipping classes again, sleeping all day and drinking all night. There is no telling what this stranger that he has become would do."

"You must be devastated by this turn of events. After all your hard work, you finally get your acceptance letter to medical school..." said Louise, letting the sentence hang in the air.

"The disappointment I feel that I'll never reach my goal of becoming a doctor pales in comparison to the sadness I feel that this child will never meet Trevor. I already love my baby more than I ever thought possible, and I'll do whatever it takes to protect this child," said Grace resolutely.

"What do you mean?"

"I need to consider adoption," Grace said with a catch in her throat.

"You can't do that! It would break your heart, Grace."

"But it's not what's best for me that matters...It's what is best for this baby." Grace stood up, excused herself, and cut through the back hallway to her room.

Louise walked back to the stove, and began stirring vigorously. Her heart ached for Grace, but it also ached for her own failed dreams. She and Charles had been trying to start a family for years, and she had all but given up hope. Louise was ashamed to admit it, but she felt resentment that it had been Grace, rather than she, who had been blessed with a child.

Louise heard the front door close, and realized Charles must be home. She wiped the tears from her eyes, and moved the pot off the stove. Dinner would have to wait. Ideas and emotions and dreams were swirling in her head, and she needed to talk to Charles before she exploded.

⸎

Grace stretched out on her bed, with her eyes closed, listening to the radio playing softly in the background. It felt so wonderful to elevate her throbbing feet after standing all day long at the bank.

She heard a knock on her door, and replied to come in. She opened her eyes to see Louise carrying a dinner tray. Louise set the tray, loaded with savory stew, corn bread muffins, and a cup of tea, on the table next to Grace's bed.

"You need some sustenance," advised Louise, as she unfolded a linen napkin over Grace's lap.

Grace sat up, and smiled. "You shouldn't have gone to all the trouble to bring me dinner in bed, but I'm mighty glad you did. I have never been as physically and emotionally exhausted as I feel at this moment."

After swallowing several large spoonfuls of the stew, energy began returning to her body.

Louise pulled a desk chair over to the bed, and sat down next to Grace. "Were you serious about considering adoption?" she asked.

Grace reached over to a framed photograph on her bedside table, and passed the portrait of Clara and Adam Dunning to Louise. "I want my baby to grow up like I did...safe, loved, happy...I'm afraid Fenton will make good on his threat to steal my baby...And even if he leaves us alone, this baby will have a tough row to hoe..."

Louise stood up and began straightening up the small room to dissipate her nervous energy. Finally, she gathered the courage to speak. "Charles and I have been talking tonight...We would like to adopt your baby and raise him or her as our own, if that would be an option you'd ever consider..."

Grace was flabbergasted. "I couldn't think of two more wonderful people to raise this child than you and Charles. Is this really something you would want to do?"

"With all my heart, Grace. I promise you that if you give us this gift, we would love this child as much as if I had given birth myself. "

They talked for over an hour about Louise's offer. Finally, Grace said, "But this would not be enough to prevent Fenton from taking me to court to claim paternity...We would have to convince the world that you delivered the baby."

"How in the world would we do that?" exclaimed Louise. "I would have to disappear from Lansing...and you would need to fake a pregnancy..."

"You could stay with my elderly aunt in Pinckney. She has a big home and doesn't socialize much, so no one would be the wiser. Do you think it would work?" asked Louise, excitedly.

"Does your cousin have a telephone? Why don't you call her tonight...If we are going to do this, I need to leave in the near future..."

Louise gave Grace a quick hug, and left the room, almost giddy. Grace rubbed her belly and a tear fell down her cheek. Her sacrifice was another woman's greatest gift, but Grace knew her little one would grow up happy with the Manns.

Grace looked around her room that had been her home for all these years and wondered if she could really abandon all the memories that made her who she was. She would be starting over in a new city, with a new name and identity, leaving behind all that mattered to her. She would be left with an empty shell of herself.

This proposed scenario would be as if she and Trevor had never existed. But was it possible that a part of them could persist in their descendents? Could any of their hopes and dreams reside somewhere deep inside her baby? Could any of the love Grace felt be remembered by the progeny she would never meet?

TWENTY-NINE

Lansing, Michigan
Saturday, February 5, 2011
7:30 AM

Dakota had spent the night since arriving home from her ill fated date with Joel watching TV Land and eating comfort food. An empty Kleenex box sat next to her. She wondered how with the ring of a doorbell, her life could have been turned upside down.

Her pride stung because she had been duped by Alex Zahn. Her anger burned because she had been falsely accused by Candace. Her anxiety swirled because she had no savings to hire a lawyer. But most importantly, her heart broke because Joel did not believe her.

As Dakota pulled another marshmallow from the bag, the door bell rang. Ignoring her red eyes, and flannel pajamas, she ran to the door, hoping to find Joel. Instead, she found Candace, looking as haggard as Dakota, standing in front of her.

"Any further communication between us will be handled by my attorney that I'll be hiring on Monday, "said Dakota, closing the door on Candace.

Candace angled her body to prevent the door from closing. "Uncle!" said Candace.

"What?"

"You've won, Dakota. I know Joel will be over later this morning... hopefully after you've showered...to beg your forgiveness. "

151

"And your purpose for coming over?"

"I suspect that you will someday become my daughter-in-law. I'd like to explain my motivations, and maybe make amends."

"I think we're getting ahead of ourselves. Joel and I are a long way from that type of a relationship."

"If you won't listen to my apologies, will you at least accept a peace offering from me? I have some information that you've been seeking... After all, I've met Grace before..."

Dakota knew she was being played, but she could not resist asking, "And what information would that be?"

"I'd rather show you. Put some clothes on and meet me in the parking lot downstairs," said Candace. She turned around and disappeared down the hallway, not bothering to wait for a reply.

As Dakota slipped on jeans and a tee-shirt, she chided herself for playing into Candace's hand. Anything Candace said would be suspect. Furthermore, Dakota was surrendering power and control by playing along. But Dakota was becoming obsessed with learning about Grace. She couldn't resist.

Ten minutes later, Dakota found herself in the passenger seat of Candace's black Cadillac Escalade. The two women sat silently as Candace turned off Michigan Avenue and headed south on Pennsylvania. The roads were still empty and covered with a layer of snow. The sun was rising in the east, and as Candace turned onto Mt. Hope Avenue, Dakota shielded her eyes from the glare.

Candace said, "We're here," and turned under the white arch of Mt. Hope Cemetery.

Dakota knew this final resting place well. She had read the historical marker several times while paying respects to family member buried here. People of interest included Ransom Eli Olds, founder of Oldsmobile and later Reo Motors, who was entombed in a family mausoleum. Lieutenant Luther Baker, who led the military in the quest to capture John Wilkes Booth, was buried here as well. Also Lucy Karney, who was born a slave, but died in 1879 a free woman at the age of 117, was also laid to rest here.

Candace drove toward the back of the cemetery and stopped the car. She grabbed a small hand held whisk broom and climbed out of the car, with Dakota following.

"Fenton came here every year on December eleventh," Candace stated.

"That's the anniversary of the fire at the Hotel Kerns. What's the significance of this area?" asked Dakota.

Candace walked over to a low lying stone on the ground and brushed off the overnight accumulation of snow. Dakota looked down at the marble slab and read the inscription out loud, "Five unidentified victims of the Hotel Kerns fire...December 11, 1934."

"Here lays Trevor Moore...inventor extraordinaire...the love of Grace's life...and your great grandfather," said Candace.

"I don't understand...Why is he buried as an unidentified victim?"

"Fenton told everyone that Trevor left town before the fire, so Trevor was not listed as part of the missing."

Dakota continued studying the stone. Who were the other nameless victims? Did they have family that wondered why they never returned home? The horror that they had endured was magnified by the indignity of their anonymity.

"Their unheard cries echo on..." whispered Dakota, her eyes moist with tears.

"Alright then... Let's move on," said Candace abruptly, heading back to the Escalade.

Dakota followed, and Candace was soon back on the road, returning along the same route. But this time, Candace veered off Pennsylvania to merge onto I-496 East.

"Where are we headed now?" asked Dakota

"Another final resting spot," said Candace.

They merged onto 127 North, and left the city limits. Dakota figured Candace would reveal the destination in her own sweet time, so she leaned back and watched the highway slip by.

"I recognized you as soon as you walked into Arnold Russell's law firm," said Candace, breaking the silence. "You're the spitting image of Grace. Quit eerie, really. For a split second, I thought I was seeing a ghost."

"Why didn't you tell me this upfront? Why do all the charades?"

"I hated Grace, and I pledged to do everything in my power to keep you out of my family."

"I'm glad we've reached an understanding that I'm no threat to you, your family or your company," said Dakota.

"Are you really that naive? You and Joel have more in common than I thought."

Dakota turned from gazing out the side window to look at Candace's expression. Instead, Dakota's eyes were drawn down to Candace's lap, where her left arm rested with a snub-nosed revolver pointed directly at Dakota.

"What the hell is going on, Candace?" demanded Dakota.

"For a supposedly intelligent woman, you're really quite daft.

I've already told you we're on our way to another final resting place."

Dakota's heart began pounding in her chest, and she felt like she couldn't breathe. Think, she told herself. This is no time to panic. She knew there would be no second chances. Keeping Candace talking would help distract her.

"Why do you hate Grace so much?" asked Dakota, as she put both hands in her coat pockets, simulating shivering.

"Fenton was obsessed with Grace, but she never gave him the time of day, unless it was convenient for her. He spent his prime years looking for her, and never would have given me a chance... as long as Grace was around."

A chill went up Dakota's spine, but she had to ask. Carefully, Dakota flipped her cell phone in her pocket to vibrate, decreased the volume, and asked, "Did you make sure Grace was not around?"

"Finally, a perceptive question! It was so easy to do. Who would have thought that a crummy job as a nurse's aide would have come in so handy."

Dakota risked a discreet peak at her right hand, dialed 911, and replaced the phone in her pocket again.

"You were the one that overdosed Grace with insulin. Her death wasn't a suicide. It was murder!" exclaimed Dakota.

"She just couldn't keep out of Fenton's life. She was contemplating a return to Lansing. I couldn't risk the chance...just like I can't risk the chance that you'll get your hooks into Joel."

"Candace, why don't you pull off 127 at this next exit for St. Johns... We can forget all of this nonsense...It would be your word against mine anyway..." pleaded Dakota.

Candace only laughed and increased her speed.

"Unless you want to see a black Escalade flipped over in the ditch, you better slow down. I bet there's black ice this morning on the highway, "Dakota yelled. She had no idea if their voices would be audible on her cell phone in her pocket, or if the 911 operator had even been reached.

"Candace, please put the gun away. I can assure you that I'm not a threat to you. I'm not trying to steal Anderson money."

Candace seemed lost in her thoughts, and Dakota doubted her words were even registering. "Don't risk everything by harming me. Even your Anderson money isn't going to help you if you kill me," said Dakota.

"Wrong again. I've spent all night planning and have all the bases covered. Philip had picked up cigarette butts and hair samples from Zand's wife, Cynthia, when he was photographing your check at her home, just in case it might come in handy some day. Planting some CSI type evidence at your final resting spot will point those investigators right toward Cynthia."

"Cynthia has a young daughter at home who needs her. You can't set her up for this!" Dakota was incensed by the ruthlessness that Candace displayed.

"Oh boo hoo. Did anyone worry about me growing up without a mother? At least the girl wasn't pimped by an alcoholic mother or locked in closets by greedy foster parents!"

Dakota had no reply for this. Candace had been scarred at such an early age. It was no wonder she lacked empathy for others. Dakota could not rely on the cavalry coming. She had to figure out another plan to get the gun away from Candace.

Farm fields flew by as the Escalade sped further north. Dakota reckoned her only chance was to wrestle the gun away from Candace while driving. Once they were out of the car, Dakota would be a sitting duck.

As Dakota was trying to get the courage to act, she became aware of a faint noise. She looked in the side view mirror and could see flashing lights in the distance. The cavalry was coming after all!

Candace also heard the siren approaching. She floored the accelerator, not willing to admit defeat. But the car was not responding. In fact, Candace felt the Escalade losing speed.

"What the hell is going on! We're slowing down!" yelled Candace.

Dakota suspected the police had slowed their vehicle through the vehicle navigational system.

"There's no way I'm going to prison! I'll never be in a closet again! Say good bye to the world, Dakota. I'll meet you in hell—"

Dakota knew she needed to act quickly. Before Candace could finish her soliloquy, Dakota's left arm shot out and slammed Candace's gun arm against the dashboard. Candace fired repeatedly, with the windshield shattering.

As the women wrestled for the gun, the Escalade veered off the highway, aiming straight towards an overpass embankment. Dakota reached over to the steering wheel and turned it sharply away from the approaching cement wall. Her last memory was of the Escalade going into a spin.

"Can you feel a pulse?" a man yelled.

"Yes, it's strong. Bring over a neck brace and a back board!" another man commanded.

Dakota's eyes blinked, trying to focus on her surroundings. I'm in a crumpled car, she told herself, as pieces of the morning started flowing back into her consciousness. Candace, she thought, where is she? Dakota rolled her eyes towards the empty driver's seat.

In the distance, Dakota heard the sharp report of a gun. Candace had kept her promise, thought Dakota…Candace would never be locked up again.

THIRTY

Lansing, Michigan
Tuesday, May 25, 1965
8:15 PM

Samuel Pierce loved his life. He had become rich by digging up dirt on one wealthy person for another. Errant husbands, crooked politicians, corrupt business men...He had done them all.

And then of course, there was his favorite meal ticket, his brother-in-law, Fenton Anderson. Fenton's obsession with finding his long lost Grace had single handedly paid for Samuel's hunting lodge in the Upper Peninsula. At first, Samuel had actually worked diligently on the case, and after a few years, he had tracked Grace to the Detroit area. But then the trail ran cold. Since then, he made regular forays into different parts of the country, but they were basically shots in the dark that gave him billable hours.

Last year, Fenton threatened to take his business elsewhere, so Samuel needed to get creative again. Then an idea hit him that seemed so simple that he was actually ashamed he had not thought of it sooner. Samuel had always surmised that Grace kept in contact with the Manns, but those people had been tight lipped for decades, regardless of how much badgering he and Fenton did. So he decided to bribe postmen to record all out-of-town return addresses on letters going to the Mann's home. It was not long before Samuel struck gold.

He looked down at his desk and saw a copy of the running report that he had given Fenton. The style of the report was not as professional looking as those produced by his secretary. Fenton had insisted that no one else know of this investigation. So Samuel had to type out the report himself. Oh well, small price to pay for a gravy train.

Maybe the most satisfying aspect of his career was how often he could play both ends against the middle. Being a double agent really broke the monotony, added a touch of intrigue, and of course doubled the paycheck.

However, not all payments were made in cash, such as today's impending transaction. Miss Candace Rogers had asked to meet him in his office, suggesting a time later in the evening, after his secretary had gone home. Candace was one of the many young women that swooned around Fenton, for his persistent good looks and of course his bank account. As usual, Fenton barely gave any of them the time of day.

Samuel thought that this woman was different from many of the vapid, empty-headed beauties Fenton seemed to attract. Candace had intelligence, and street smarts, along with sex appeal oozing out from every inch of her overly tight dresses. Candace had been sniffing around Samuel lately, and he was not dumb enough to think she had the hots for him. She wanted something from him, and he suspected it was the contents of this report on Grace.

Candace had been Fenton's date at a recent charity event hosted by Anderson Technologies. Samuel's sweet but constantly gabbing wife had filled Candace in on all of the gory details of the relationship between Fenton and Grace. Ever since, Candace had been making goo-goo eyes at Samuel.

Well, could he help it if Candace accidently sees this report lying on his desk? Of course, that would occur after a very thorough "investigation" took place on his large leather couch.

Samuel leaned back in his chair and smiled. Someday, he would pass on his kingdom to his son, Philip. Yes, Samuel had a great life indeed.

THIRTY-ONE

Dakota unlocked her condominium door, and Dr. Everett followed her in. "Thanks again for the ride home. Have a seat, and I'll make us some tea."

Dakota had been hospitalized for overnight observation following her head concussion. Upon discharge, she had found herself with no way back to Lansing. Morgan and her family were due back today from a Caribbean cruise, and Dakota did not want to dampen their vacation with the horror of her drive with Candace. When Dr. Everett had called to set up their next testing session, he had been quite upset to learn of her brain trauma. He had insisted on chauffeuring her home himself.

While putting the kettle on the stove, Dakota peaked at her cell phone to see if Joel had called her. She had tried to call him last night from the hospital, but his phone had been turned off. Joel must be hurting, losing his mother in such horrible circumstances. Disappointed that there was no message, Dakota left the phone on the counter and excused herself to get washed up while the water boiled.

Hearing the vibration of her cell phone, Dr. Everett walked over to the counter to see a missed call had been received from Joel Anderson. Dr. Everett deleted the call, and set about pouring the boiling water over tea bags in the mugs.

Dakota walked back into the kitchen, refreshed from splashing water on her face. She moved into the living room, where her tea awaited her.

"I've discovered so much about the origins of my dreams since we last talked," said Dakota, sitting down in an overstuffed chair.

"Do tell," said Dr. Everett, opening his notebook on the coffee table in front of him.

"The unsettling discovery is that I'm not biologically related to Morgan and Aunt Charity. My grandmother Charlotte was adopted in secret. Charlotte's biological mother was Grace Dunning, who witnessed the fire at the Hotel Kerns, and Charlotte's biological father was Trevor Moore, who perished in the tragedy. " Dakota filled Dr. Everett in on the details of her discoveries, omitting the budding romance that had occurred between her and Joel.

"And what were Morgan's and Charity's reactions to this news?" he asked.

Dakota paused and averted his eyes. "Um, I've been so busy that I haven't had a chance to fill them in yet."

Dr. Everett sat in silence for several minutes. The only sign of movement was his foot slowly tapping the ground. When he spoke, his tone was flat. "I seem to remember telling you not to look into this matter, that it would alter our data collection. You don't follow directions very well, do you Dr. Graham?"

Dakota blushed, feeling like a child reprimanded. She honestly had forgotten this admonition in her enthusiasm to get some answers.

"Are you serious about this research or not? I don't have time to play games with you, and I'm not putting my reputation on the line with a test subject that is subverting our research!" he blustered, with his face turning red.

"I am very serious about this research. I realize now that I'm witnessing the actual life experiences of my ancestor, that these are Grace's real memories!"

"Let me ask you a question, Dr. Graham...Since you have made these discoveries, how have your so called dreams changed?" asked Dr. Everett.

Now Dakota sat silently, trying to remember her last dream. Until this moment, she had not realized that no daytime or nighttime dreams had occurred since her journey to Savannah. In fact, the normal anxiety she experienced just thinking about the dreams had been replaced with a fascination and a passion to explore them more fully.

"Precisely," said Dr. Graham, not waiting for an answer. "We believe memories of every day events are stored in neuronal networks in the hippocampus of the brain. Reactivating these networks is how we remember. But these circuits are affected by many factors, including the passage of time, and thus most memories fade or disappear as we age."

Dr. Everett finished drinking his tea before he continued. "But these ancestral memories that we both have experienced are different. These memories remain sharp and fresh throughout the years... that is, until we start placing them into historical context."

"What do you mean?"

"Once I read the writings of my ancestor, learned about his revolutionary beliefs that challenged the establishment thinking in England, researched his sham trial and subsequent hanging, my memories changed....They were no longer crisp, reliable, painfully brutal. They became hazy, patchy, like a normal memory does with the passage of time. When ancestral memories are matched to real life scenarios, they cease to be hard wired, and start to fade like everyday memories."

Dakota didn't know whether to be relieved or sad. These memories had been so much a part of her life for so long. Now that she knew the memories were her connection to Grace, she felt a sense of loss that the images would be fading.

"How long before the memories fade?" Dakota asked.

"They already have...We have very little time left if you are serious about unlocking this mystery. So are you willing to do what it takes?" he asked.

Dakota sat wondering what to do next. Since she had started this journey, her life had become unraveled. Maybe it was best to walk away at this point. Dr. Everett seemed to sense her hesitation as well and said, "You'll regret it if you pass up a chance to unlock a mystery that could rock our understanding of human memory."

She had never been a quitter. She knew she had to see this journey to the end, no matter where it led her. "What will it take, Dr Everett?" she asked, resolutely.

"We need to stop distractions, as well as any contact with pertinent historical information. We need to optimize the time remaining...Are you willing to devote yourself full time to this project?" he asked.

Dakota thought of all her responsibilities. She would have to find a substitute doctor for her practice. Her family would have to shoulder her share of visiting Grandma Charlotte in the nursing home. She would not be available to support Joel in his grieving, assuming he wanted anything to do with her at this point.

"I have a retired colleague that might agree to fill in for me for a couple weeks..."

"You start making your necessary calls to your medical associates. But call Morgan later tonight. If you don't dally, there'll still be time today for some investigations," commanded Dr. Everett, as if Dakota's mind were already made up.

Forty minutes later, Dakota was surprised how everything had fallen into place. Her colleague was at loose ends, with his wife out of town visiting grandkids. He had jumped at the chance to see patients again. When she called her staff about her plans to take some time off, they had assumed the purpose was to recover from the ordeal with Candace that had made the front page of the State Journal that morning. Dakota did not correct them, keeping her work with Dr. Everett to herself.

Dr. Everett handed her another cup of tea and sat down next to her, with his notebook open on his lap. "Let me map out our protocol for the next two weeks to maximize our remaining time."

Dakota sipped on her hot tea in hopes of calming her nerves, but it was to no avail. She had an overwhelming sense of heading out into turbulent waters, without having a life jacket.

THIRTY-TWO

Savannah, Georgia
Tuesday, June 15, 1965
10:35 AM

G race had been procrastinating for several weeks, but today she had made up her mind to answer Louise's letter. Ever since receiving mail from Lansing, Grace had been wrestling with her conscience. On the one hand, being a part of Charlotte's life would be a dream come true. On the other hand, Grace was not convinced disrupting Charlotte's life was the best outcome for her daughter.

Grace thought back to the world in 1935, in the middle of the Great Depression, a much different time for women than in the 1960's. It was easy to forget that women had the right to vote for only fifteen years prior to Charlotte's birth, and that legal protection against discrimination toward women had only been passed last year with the Civil Rights Act. Sometimes in the stillness of the night, Grace would lie awake and wondered... Would she have made the same decision and opted for adoption had Charlotte been born in 1965?

No more delaying, thought Grace. It was time to collect her thoughts and put them down on paper. Her poor eye sight was an additional hurdle for composing the letter. Grace relied on magnifying glasses and typewriters for her correspondences. She rolled a sheet of typing paper into the carriage, and got down to work.

The barking of her Golden Retriever Abbey alerted her to company arriving minutes before the door bell rang. Grace pulled out her letter from the typewriter and placed the sheet in a folder, away from prying eyes. She had kept her secret safe for thirty years by maintaining a high level of vigilance.

Abbey was already at the door, her entire rear end moving back in forth in excitement for a visitor. Grace opened the door and found a man standing there.

"Grace...You're as beautiful as ever," the man said softly.

The man's face was blurry, but Grace remembered the voice well. Without hesitating, she flung her arms around Fenton's neck and hugged him, saying, "Then your eyes are as bad as mine... Oh, how I've missed you!"

Fenton followed Grace into the front parlor room, with Abbey's head bumping up against Fenton's hand, demanding some attention too. "I've dreamed of this day for thirty years, but I expected a door to be slammed in my face," said Fenton.

Grace smiled, and said, "Have a seat, Fenton. We've both grown up and matured, I'm sure, since our last conversation... You have no idea how wonderful it is to be with someone who remembers Grace Dunning." Her eyes misted over, remembering the heartache of reinventing herself.

"You didn't make it easy to find you. My brother-in-law pretty much had a full time job all these years looking for your trail... I came over to the boarding house the day after I said those hateful things to you to beg your forgiveness...But you had already vanished into thin air..."

"I know you did..."

"And I pestered Louise regularly over the years, because I was convinced you would stay in touch with her..."

Abbey seemed to sense Fenton's sadness, laying her head in his lap with her soulful eyes gazing up at him.

"Grace...What happened to your baby?"

Grace hesitated before answering. "Grew up in a wonderful family, and is leading a fulfilling life."

"It's my fault that you had to resort to adoption."

"Your threats certainly increased my sense of urgency... But I was already thinking long and hard that adoption would

Be the best option for her."

"A little girl! I bet she is just like her mommy," Trevor said wistfully. "Will you tell me who raised her? "

Grace petted Abbey for a long time in silence, before finally replying, "If I tell you, will you promise never to interfere in my daughter's life as long as you live?"

"I swear, Grace."

"Then I'll tell you my story...if you tell me the real story of what happened to Trevor."

"I've been looking for you all these years to do just that..."

THIRTY-THREE

Ann Arbor, Michigan
Sunday, February 6, 2011
11:40 PM

W hen Dakota opened her eyes, she felt a wave of nausea wash over her. She sat up to vomit, but an explosion of pain inside her head dropped her to the bed again.

For the second time in twenty-four hours, Dakota tried to piece together the fragments of memories in her brain. She remembered sustaining a concussion when Candace's car careened off US-27. And later, Dr. Everett had driven her home from the emergency room. But the last thing she remembered was drinking a cup of tea in her living room with Dr. Everett.

How did she end up in bed, still dressed, but with her comforter over her? Possibly her concussion had been worse than originally diagnosed. Could she have a delayed intracranial bleed from the trauma?

She felt anxious and unsettled, and knew something was very wrong. She needed to get help. The room had very dim lighting which contributed to her disorientation. She slowly rolled onto her side, and then pushed herself to a sitting position. The room was spinning, and her arms and legs seemed clumsy.

The bright light from an opening door made Dakota shield her eyes in pain, but not before identifying the silhouette of Dr. Everett. "I thought I heard you waking up," he said.

"Am...glad...you...here...need...help...need... hospital..." Dakota struggled to get her words out.

"You'll be fine, Dr. Graham. You're just suffering from a little hangover. The motor weakness, speech problems, and dizziness will all resolve, but I doubt your memory of today will return. Now, go back to bed and sleep it off. Tomorrow, you'll be your old self again."

Her confusion was only increasing at this point. The room was becoming in focus now, and despite recognizing some of her belongings, this was not her bedroom.

"How...get here?"

"With a little help of Rohypnol and my automobile."

Dakota's forehead furrowed as she tried with all her might to remember that word. "Date rape drug!" she finally yelled, and instinctively pulled the comforter around her.

"Relax, Dr. Graham...You're not my type. Besides, I'm only interested in your mind," he said with a condescending laugh. "You're going to be my guest here at Souviens. You've clearly proven you are unreliable and can't follow directions. You've left me no choice than to spike your tea. You'll be sequestered here for the duration of our research."

"You...can't force me..." she stammered out, with great frustration.

"Oh, that's where I beg to differ, Dr. Graham. You're forgetting I know where two adorable twin boys live...And I seem to remember seeing the name of their grade school on the refrigerator door. I'm not a violent man by nature, but I am on a mission...a mission much greater than you and I. And I will use all the tools at my disposal to get you to cooperate."

His blatant threat caused fear to surge through her body, and she could feel her right arm beginning to burn. She unconsciously began rubbing her right arm as the memory of burning debris hitting her arm ramped up. Looking pleased, Dr. Everett said, "I see my tactics are working already to stimulate your memories. Too bad we're not imaging your brain right now."

Dr. Everett walked into her room and turned on a night light. "So we won't attract attention, your night time lighting will be limited. But you'll find your accommodations quite comfortable. I took the liberty of bringing some items from your home that might be needed... your purse...your own comforter and pillow...some clean clothes and cosmetics....But don't bother looking for any electronics. Now we have a busy day tomorrow, so I suggest you get some rest."

Dakota clutched herself tightly in her blanket as Dr. Everett walked out the door. He pulled a keychain out of his pocket, and placed a key into the door deadbolt as he turned around to look at Dakota.

"Have you ever heard of a man name Henry Molaison?" asked Dr. Everett in a cold, flat tone.

Dakota shook her head no.

"Poor Henry suffered from unrelenting epilepsy. He underwent an experimental surgery where the hippocampus area of the brain was removed. The epilepsy improved, but he lost the ability to form long term memories from that point on. Much was learned about memory from his willingness to be studied over the years. And when he died, he donated his brain for continued research..."

Dakota's eyes opened very wide as she began to understand Dr. Everett's agenda.

"I happened to have noticed when you showed your driver's license to security that you also designated your body to scientific research upon your death...Of course, one would expect that a young, healthy woman such as yourself has decades of living ahead of herself...unless something unforeseen were to happen...You see, Dr. Graham, I have many options available to me for furthering my research."

THIRTY-FOUR

Savannah, Georgia
Tuesday, June 15, 1965
2:10 PM

Candace Rogers had no game plan, no scheme. She only knew that the woman living in this home stood between her and a meal ticket. She figured the first step was to know thy enemy.

Candace had followed Fenton to Savannah, thanks to help from the private investigator report found on Samuel Pierce's desk. Fenton had left Grace's home about thirty minutes ago, after a three hour long visit. The coast appeared clear, and it was time to make a move.

As Candace climbed the porch steps, a dog began barking inside. Great, she thought. She hated dogs, and the feeling was usually mutual. Candace remembered the mongrel that her foster mother had coddled like a princess, while Candace often went hungry.

Before Candace could ring the doorbell, the door opened, with a golden retriever bounding out to great her.

"Since you came back for your hat, maybe now you'll stay for dinner," announced the woman following the dog.

Candace guessed that the woman, with short salt and pepper hair, no makeup, and Capri pants, must be the housekeeper. "Can you please control your dog? I'm looking for Grace Davis."

"Abbey, sit...I'm Grace. How can I help you?"

Candace was left speechless. This pale and thin looking woman, with clearly no fashion sense, simply could not be the love of Fenton's life. "Um...I'm a friend of Fenton's...He sent me here to collect his hat."

"Please, come on in. Sorry about Abbey. She thinks everyone wants to be her friend."

Candace followed Grace back into the home. The front parlor looked comfortable enough, in a middle class sort of way. But Candace had her decorating standards set higher, with no furniture from local department stores allowed.

Grace ran into the edge of an ottoman and tripped. This woman was as graceful, as she was stylish, thought Candace.

"I'm such a klutz since my vision began deteriorating," Grace said, as she picked herself up. "Here's Fenton's hat...So, how do you know Fenton?"

Taking the hat, Candace said, "We met when I was working as a model at the Detroit Auto Show. We've been dating ever since. In fact, I met his entire family at an Anderson Company party," Candace bragged. So what if the party was their only date, Candace thought.

"How wonderful. Well, it's nice to meet you...I'm sorry, I didn't catch your name."

"Candace."

"Maybe I'll see you again back in Michigan. I've been thinking about a trip home. It may be overdue."

Candace felt a surge of panic. Somehow she needed to dissuade Grace from returning to Lansing. Candace began subtly swaying.

Are you feeling ok?" asked Grace.

"Just a little light headed from this Georgia heat...May I use your restroom?"

"Please, help yourself. It's right through the kitchen. And pour yourself some ice tea that is in the refrigerator on your way back."

Candace disappeared into the kitchen to regroup, leaving Grace and Abbey in the parlor. Fenton must have said something to get the reluctant Grace to return home. Was it a promise of a new relationship? The private investigator's report never mentioned a baby, but Fenton's sister had said everyone surmised the pregnant Grace had placed the child up for adoption. Did Grace's return have anything to do with that child? Candace knew there was no hope of breaking Fenton's obsession if Grace returned to Lansing. She had to figure out Grace's Achilles' heel.

That glass of ice tea might help clear her head. Setting Fenton's hat on the counter, Candace opened the refrigerator door and pulled out a tall pitcher. As she was about to close the door, something caught her eye. On the top refrigerator shelf was a metal tray with several prefilled syringes. She picked up the adjacent vile, labeled NPH insulin.

Candace remembered the last time she had seen such a vial was while working as a nurse's aide. Usually her responsibilities revolved around bed pans and urinals. But occasionally, she would help the nurses dispense medications. One night stood out in her memory when hospital food had been particularly unpalatable earlier that day. Mr. Murphy in the room across from the nursing station had silently protested the cuisine by throwing out all his food. His fast was unbeknownst to his nurse, who proceeded to give him his full dosage of insulin for the day. By the end of her shift, Mr. Murphy had a seizure and almost died.

Candace replaced the medical supplies in the refrigerator, and poured herself some ice tea. She swirled the liquid in the glass and tried to figure out what Grace had that she lacked. Why had she never been loved passionately? She searched her memory but could never remember even feeling loved. For that matter, she never remembered loving anybody else either.

A feeling of hatred was growing inside of Candace towards Grace. Grace didn't deserve Fenton. Grace was too old to give him an heir, and had deserted him for decades. Candace may not be as educated as the woman who was accepted to medical school all those years ago, but Candace had learned quite a bit in school before she had dropped out. One of the theories discussed in her biology class was echoing in her memory..."Survival of the fittest"...She sensed that concept may be apropos to her current situation.

She set the glass down and returned to the refrigerator. Her hand rested on the handle a long time before opening the door. She knew that there was no turning back if she went down this route. Picking up the tray and the vial, she retreated to the bathroom to do her handiwork.

After several minutes, Candace jumped when Grace knocked on the door, and said, "Everything okay in there?"

"I'm feeling a lot better. Be out in just a bit," Candace's hand was shaking as she substantially increased the insulin in one of the syringes, discarding the other ones in her pocket. With Grace's poor eye sight, Candace was betting she would never notice the difference.

Now the problem was moving the supplies back to the refrigerator and getting the hell out of Dodge before being seen by anyone else. She peeked outside the bathroom door and could hear Grace in the parlor, playing with the dog. With her heart pounding, Candace quickly replaced the tray and vial, and gulped down some ice tea to quench her dry mouth. She grabbed Fenton's hat and moved into the parlor.

"Thanks for letting me freshen up. I'll be on my way now," said Candace, moving purposefully towards the door.

"Are you feeling better?"

"Much...Let's do lunch if you decide to visit Lansing," Candace hollered over her shoulder, never making eye contact with Grace again.

Once outside, Candace quickly walked several streets over to catch a city bus. Wearing dark sunglasses, she settled into a seat, and looked at the buildings passing by.

A strange sensation began to stir in her. It brought a smile to her face, and lifted her spirits considerably. Eventually, she identified the feeling. After all these years, Candace finally felt loved and supported. The rest of world may have abandoned her, but Candace Rogers knew that she could always rely on herself to guarantee survival of the fittest.

THIRTY-FIVE

Lansing, Michigan
Monday, February 7, 2011
7:50 AM

Morgan took a swig from her coffee, hoping the caffeine would see her through the full schedule today. Her family had missed their connecting flight in Miami and had ended up in Detroit at midnight. Only a few hours of sleep had left her with a nagging headache.

Morgan had promised herself after their vacation that she would sit down with Dakota for a much needed tete-a-tete. During a long walk on the beach, her husband had convinced Morgan that her insecurities about Dakota's family ties were baseless. He felt that Morgan owed it to Dakota to be honest with her. The lying would do more damage to their relationship than their dissimilar DNA.

Morgan pushed those worries aside until lunch when she would call Dakota, and began focusing on getting her physical therapy center ready for a busy Monday. Her partner was due to arrive any minute, so when Morgan heard the door open, she hollered, "Hey Paula, do you have any Motrin for my throbbing headache?"

"No, but I'd be happy to run across the street to the pharmacy for you."

Her head snapped up when she heard a male voice.

"You're clearly not Paula. How may I help you, sir?" Morgan asked.

"Are you Dakota's cousin?" he asked.

"Yes, I am… And you are?" asked Morgan, somewhat leerily.

"Please excuse me for being rude. I'll blame it on lack of sleep. I'm Joel Anderson…I'm surely the last person you want to see today…I'm just really worried about Dakota. If you can tell me that she's okay, I'll leave you all alone."

Morgan realized this was another example of the cousins' fraying relationship. In the past, Morgan would have been old friends by now with Dakota's special man. But thanks to the lie between them, Morgan had found excuses not to have had Joel over for dinner yet.

"Hey, it's great to meet you. I've heard so many wonderful things about you. Please, come in. Would you like a cup of coffee? And what's this about being worried for Dakota?" The words came tumbling out quickly in a caffeine induced frenzy.

Joel was somewhat taken aback at Morgan's friendliness. Given Joel's betrayal when his mother had hurled the nasty allegations at Dakota, and then his mother's subsequent kidnapping attempt, he had expected to be hanged, drawn and quartered by Morgan without a trial. Dakota had told him how her older cousin had always been her protector.

But before Joel could explain, a woman walked in the door, yelling "Morgan, what in the world are you doing here today? I've already rearranged your patients to fit into my schedule. You need to go home to Dakota."

"Paula, this is Morgan's friend Joel Anderson…And what am I missing here? What's going on with Dakota?" Morgan's voice was filled with palpable anxiety.

If looks could kill, Joel knew Paula would have succeeded. "Man, you have some explaining to do. " And with that, Paula pulled the Lansing State Journal out of her bag, with the bold headlines blaring, "Wealthy Heiress Kidnaps Local Doctor".

Morgan felt like she had been kicked in the gut. While she had been having fun in the sun, Dakota's world was being tipped upside down. Joel had told Morgan that he had gone over to Dakota's condominium to apologize Saturday morning. He had seen her car in the parking lot, and when Dakota had not answered his repeated knocking on the door, he had left, respecting her wishes to be alone. It was only later that he realized her home had been empty, and that Dakota had been on the fateful ride with his mother.

That evening, the police had called Joel to make the identification of his mother's body after Candace had shot herself. Then the police had played the 911 recording for him that Dakota had ingeniously made.

When Joel went to see Dakota in the hospital, she had already been released. Again, he found her car in the condominium's parking lot, but she was not answering her phone or her door. Now, Joel wanted to make sure she was safe before he left her alone.

So Morgan found herself following Joel's truck as they drove towards Dakota's home. And if Dakota did not answer the door this time, Morgan had a spare key to use.

J oel was struggling to control his emotions and told himself to concentrate on the road ahead. In the last forty-eight hours, his mother had kidnapped the love of his life, only to end up killing herself. Despite her verbal abuse over the years, Joel had loved his mother, excusing her behavior due to her horrific childhood and loveless marriage. Her actions this weekend, however, were unforgiveable.

He did not deserve Dakota's love for allowing his mother to harm her. Had Joel stood up to his mother Friday night, Dakota would have been safe in his home, eating his scrambled eggs Saturday morning, rather than hurtling down US 27 with a murderer. He had no right to ask for Dakota's forgiveness at this point. But Joel had a nagging sense that Dakota was still not safe. He would not rest until proven otherwise.

Morgan opened Dakota's condominium with her spare key, and Joel followed her inside. The living room had that empty sound that no one notices until someone is missing.

"Before stopping to see you, I went to her office. Her staff wouldn't talk to me, but a patient in the parking lot told me that a fellow physician was filling in for a couple weeks," said Joel. "Do you think Dakota could simply have left town without her car?"

"Dakota wouldn't leave town for an extended period of time without touching base with me. Between my husband, my mother, Dakota and me, someone visits Charlotte daily in the nursing home. Dakota would never leave without rearranging that schedule. No... Something is amiss...I can feel it."

Morgan started slowly walking through Dakota's condominium, looking for anything out of place or missing. She opened closets and cupboards, and leafed through piles of paper on Dakota's desk before returning to the living room.

Morgan sat down on the couch and rubbed her throbbing temples. "Several things stick out as weird...nothing earth shattering, but weird... Her bed pillow and comforter are gone...Her electric tooth brush is missing, along with the bottle of shampoo usually in the shower...And the two mugs that my boys gave her are in the cupboard, instead of their usual place of prominence, hanging from the hooks on the wall," mused Morgan out loud. "But her suitcase is still in the closet, and her cell phone is turned off and sitting on the counter."

"I think we need to call the police," said Joel.

"They aren't going to do anything. She has only been missing a day now, and she told her staff she needed a break. The authorities will assume she did just that, and left town...No, it's up to us to figure this out... How did she get home from the hospital up North anyway?"

"Don't know...I think we need to check her car. Do you have a spare car key as well?" asked Joel.

Morgan was addicted to television crime shows, and felt nauseated at the thought of opening the car trunk. She grabbed her keys, and they both headed out the door in silence. As they were walking down the stairwell, an older man passed them, carrying bags of groceries. On a whim, Joel asked, "Excuse me, sir. Do you by any chance know Dakota Graham who lives on the next floor up?"

"Sure, I know Dak. We're baseball buddies and go to Lugnuts games together...I hope she's feeling better today," he said.

"I'm her cousin Morgan. You must be George."

"Hey, Morgan, finally we meet. Terrible thing that happened to Dak on Saturday. I guess I'd tip a few back if someone tried to kill me too."

"What do you mean?" asked Morgan.

"She was three sheets to the wind yesterday, if you get my drift."

"George, I really need to find Dakota. Please tell me everything you saw yesterday," pleaded Morgan.

"Well, I was getting out of my car in the parking lot when I saw Dak walking arm and arm with a man about my age...thinner build, with sparse gray hair. She was pretty wobbly, slurring her words...I don't think she even recognized me when I said hello. He put her in his Toyota, and then drove away."

Morgan thanked George for his help, and promised to let him know when Dakota was located. Once George was out of earshot, Morgan said, "Did Dakota ever mention to you a man named Dr. Theo Everett?"

"No...Do you think Dakota got into this Dr. Everett's car?"

"I think Dr. Everett may have succeeded where your mother failed. I have my computer in my car. We need to find a Wi-Fi spot, and search for this SOB...Damn it, I should have decked him when I had the chance," swore Morgan.

THIRTY-SIX

Savannah, Georgia
Tuesday, June 15, 1965
4:20 PM

T he hotel bar was empty, and Fenton sat alone in a booth, nursing his cola. He had not touched alcohol or cigarettes since Grace left in 1935. He had not even craved them...until today. In some ways, the weight of the world had been taken off his shoulders. Grace had forgiven him...for all his lies, his insults, his immaturity. But in other ways, he had to witness the outcome of his actions first hand. His beloved Grace was all alone in the world, dealing with failing health, without the love and support of her daughter and the love of her life, Trevor Moore.

A waitress stopped by Fenton's table to check on him. He paid his bill, deciding a bar was probably not the safest place for him right now. At forty-nine years old, it was time for him to figure out what he wanted to do when he grew up...Perhaps a city park would be a better place for reflection.

Fenton had put all his energy into building Anderson Technologies. While he had numerous superficial flings with women over the years, he had never let any of them too get serious. Today, Grace had urged him to consider starting a family and having children. Fenton had never allowed himself to think he was worthy of pursuing those things.

Fenton reached for this hat, but the table was empty. He then remembered leaving his hat on Grace's ottoman. Was that a sign that

Fenton should go back to her home? Maybe this time he could convince Grace to return to Lansing with him.

He threw a tip on the table and stood up to leave. He noted that there was now another bar patron. A stunning young woman with perfectly coiffed blonde hair, a pearl necklace, and a form fitting turquoise cocktail dress was sitting by herself at the end of the room. She was the spitting image of Candace, a woman he had taken to a company party earlier in the year. A colleague had introduced him to the model at the Detroit Auto Show in January. By the end of the company party, her breathtaking beauty had been overshadowed by the inner coldness Fenton had sensed. He had never called her again, although she had left several messages for him.

Better to duck out the rear entrance, he thought, just by some unlikely chance the woman was really Candace, but his plan was too late. The woman had already made eye contact with him and was walking towards his table.

"Fenton! What in the world are you doing down in Savannah, Georgia?"

"Hello Candace. Just visiting a friend. And you?"

"I just completed a modeling assignment. Why don't we have dinner together, and you can tell me why you haven't answered any of my messages I've left, you naughty boy. "

She kissed his cheek, linked her arm with his, and escorted him to the dining room. Once they were seated, the waiter came to take their drink orders, and said, "For the lady?"

"Dry Martini."

"And for the gentleman?"

"I'll have a glass of ice tea, please."

"Come now, Fenton. Don't be such a dull boy. Live a little!" said Candace after the waiter had left. She pulled a cigarette out of her case and waited for Fenton to light it for her.

Ignoring her cigarette, he said, "Alcohol and I don't mix very well. Will you excuse me for a moment?" Fenton retreated to the solace of the washroom, cursing himself for being roped into this dinner.

The waiter returned with their drinks, and a basket of bread sticks. Candace peaked over her shoulder, and then pulled the ice tea closer to her. She removed a small container from her purse and dumped a fine white powdery substance into the tall glass. She stirred

Fenton's drink with her swivel sticks before sliding the glass back. She lit her cigarette, and inhaled deeply, calming her nerves and sharpening her mind.

She had almost finished her martini and cigarette before Fenton returned. "Better drink your ice tea before the cubes melt in this heat," said Candace.

Fenton placed a spoon in his glass and mixed the contents, and said, "Candace, I'm not going to be able to stay for dinner. After we finish our drinks, I have someone I need to see tonight." He then took a large swig of his ice tea.

Candace chewed on her olive for awhile, and then took a sip of her martini. "So Fenton, who were you visiting here in Savannah?"

"An old family friend."

"Does this friend have children?"

Fenton was suddenly feeling very warm, despite sitting under a large ceiling fan. He removed his seersucker jacket and wiped his sweaty forehead with his handkerchief.

"She raised her stepson."

"No children of her own?"

Fenton's mouth felt parched and he took another large swallow of his ice tea.

"She placed the child up for adoption after the father died in a terrible fire."

What was he doing, wondered Fenton, telling a virtual stranger Grace's intimate history. He was feeling very dizzy and on the verge of vomiting.

"Candace, I'm not feeling well at all. I need to leave now. His words sounded slurred and distant in his ears.

"Of course, Fenton. Let me help you to your feet. This Georgia heat is getting the best of you, I think."

The waiter came over to the table to offer assistance, after seeing Fenton struggling to stand. Candace said, "Mr. Anderson is feeling under the weather. Charge the drinks to his account. Would you be a dear and call a taxis for us?"

⌘

As soon as Fenton opened his eyes, his head felt squeezed, as if in a vice. His mouth felt like sandpaper. The bright sunshine pouring in the windows prompted him to close his eyes again.

He could not place his surroundings. The room appeared to be one of the numerous generic hotel suites he had visited as a businessman. He slowly rolled over in bed, and opened his eyes again. His heart skipped a beat when he realized he was not alone in the bed. Blond locks cascaded down a shapely naked back of a woman lying next to him.

Hangovers were commonplace in his drinking days, but Fenton had never blacked out before. His last memory was of looking for his hat in the bar, and then seeing the woman that looked like Candace across the room from him.

The woman began to stir and rolled over towards Fenton. "Morning, Lover. How are you feeling?" she asked.

"Candace...How did we get here?"

"You certainly tied one on last night in celebration, but don't tell me that you've forgotten our first night together as man and wife?" Candace flashed a huge rock on her left hand as if to offer scientific proof.

Fenton's mouth dropped open, but no words came out. The only thing that made sense, he thought, was that he was either in the Twilight Zone or in Hell. And given his track record over the years, the latter was the more likely scenario.

THIRTY-SEVEN

Ann Arbor, Michigan
Monday, February 21, 2011
8:40 PM

Dakota had lost track of the number of days since her captivity. Dr. Everett had filled most of her days, as well as nights, with various testing protocols, and consequently, her circadian rhythm was totally disrupted. Sleep deprivation is often used for torture, and it was starting to take its toll on Dakota.

She had seen no opportunities for escaping or for signally for help. Dr. Everett had told her many times that she could scream all she liked, as the walls were sound proof at Souviens. No visitors ever popped into Dr. Everett's lab as he was clearly an antisocial narcissist, who had insisted on privacy for years.

The intense stress she had been under had triggered her memories of the Hotel Kerns fire on a daily basis. If there were a saving grace, Dr. Everett was thrilled with his data collection. He had captured her "dreams" with the functional MRI, a sleep study, an EEG, and a PET scan. At least he was no longer threatening harm to her family. But one of these days, he would run out of noninvasive tests to run. Would he then resort to the ultimate experiment with her brain?

She shook off the chill running up her spine and refused to let her mind wander to that possibility. Dr. Everett had given her a reprieve from testing because he had a "dog and pony show", as he called it, for Venture Capitalists today. The light was disappearing from her only window to the world, and she wondered if he would be back tonight for more testing.

Her legs ached from the long hours of lying still for testing. She should run on the elliptical machine next to her bed, but she was emotionally and physically exhausted. She glanced at the mounted camera on the wall over the bathroom door, and wondered if she were again under the microscope. Being constantly observed like another one of his lab animals was driving her insane. Dakota was on the verge of screaming, crying, or both, but she refused to give Dr. Everett the pleasure. She decided to retreat to her only island of privacy, the bathroom.

She grabbed her purse, some clean underwear and a towel, pretending she was preparing to shower. She entered the bathroom, turned on the shower, and sat on the toilet lid to cry, with her sobs camouflaged by the sound of running water.

Oh God, she thought, here I am again, asking for your help. I'm sure you're tired of people forgetting about you until they're in a scrape. She blew her nose with the toilet paper and continued to pray. Well, I'm in a real pickle right now. Please show me a way out.

She looked up at her narrow window to the world. The night was particularly dark. No stars could be seen. Her mind flashed to happier days when she and Morgan would camp out in Grandma Charlotte's back yard. Of course, the cousins were never simply in a back yard. Their imaginations placed them all over the globe, from a safari in Africa to a ship on the ocean.

She remembered the times they used flash lights to signal Morse code to each other in the darkened back yard. The girls had spent hours practicing the dots and dashes alphabet until their batteries had run out or until Grandma Charlotte had called them in for the night.

Dakota looked down at her purse in her lap and wondered... Was it possible? Her friends would laugh at her purse, more aptly labeled a sack with straps. Her purse was always the go-to spot on a scavenger hunt. And she always had her six inch Maglite flashlight in the bottom. Could Dr. Everett have left it there?

She rummaged around the bag in the dark until her hands ran across the metal cylindrical object. Could this idea possibly work?

She set her belongings on the floor and climbed up onto the toilet tank lid. Luckily she was a light weight or she would have a broken toilet to explain. She prayed the batteries were not old, aimed the Maglite out her portal, and began the international signal for SOS.

Three short flashes, three long flashes, three short flashes, followed by a pause. She continued until her arm was tired, and she became worried that the prolonged shower would cause attention. She climbed down and turned off the water, after dampening the towel for good measure.

With fresh clothes on, she climbed into her bed, hoping to be left alone tonight. She glanced up at the darkened window again, and tried to remember the area surrounding Souviens. She could only remember some other businesses set quite a distance down the road, which were sure to be empty this time of night anyway. What a childish act the flashlight signals had been. She was not in Grandma's back yard anymore. She closed her eyes tight to block out the darkness and her tears.

It had been almost two weeks since Dakota had disappeared. Morgan had eventually gone to the police, on Joel's insistence, but as she predicted, no missing person report was taken. If Dr. Graham did not return to work at the end of her two week hiatus, Morgan had been told to file a report at that time.

In the meantime, Morgan, her husband, and Joel had taken shifts following Dr. Everett's every move. Morgan had decided early on that it would not be productive to confront Dr. Everett about his involvement with Dakota's disappearance. He would only deny and deflect any accusations. More importantly, he would know they were on to him.

His activities were bizarre, going back and forth from his home to Souviens at all hours of day and night. She did not know when this man ever slept, but still there were no signs of Dakota.

Tonight, Joel had decided to take the investigation up a notch and break into Dr. Everett's home. Joel had just called Morgan to let her know that Dr. Everett was leaving the conference center and was making a bee line back to Souviens. At that point, Morgan would take over the surveillance, while Joel would return to Dr. Everett's home to look for clues.

Morgan could hear her mother's voice warning that breaking the law was never the right choice. But Morgan and Joel were desperate and running out of time. There was no doubt in her mind that Dr. Everett was up to no good. But her biggest worry was what he would do once Dakota was no longer any use to him.

It helped that Dr. Everett was a creature of habit, and always parked his Toyota in the same spot every night. She had parked her vehicle in a strip mall located behind Souviens, and was standing in cluster of trees, binoculars in tow, watching for his arrival.

It was very dark tonight, no moon or stars in the sky. Morgan had a flashback to all the dark nights she and Dakota spent in Charlotte's back yard, making up all sorts of crazy scenarios. Sticks in the yard were makeshift swords...The patio deck was a fortress to defend... Their red Flyer wagon was a stage coach. She often thought how video games and computers were limiting the imaginative play of children compared to past generations.

Deep in thought, Morgan almost missed a faint flash of light coming from the far south end of the Souviens building. It must have been her imagination, she thought, and looked back towards the parking lot at the north end of the building...But there it was again, a flash out of the corner of her eye. Ok, she thought, let's focus on the south side of the building and put this matter to rest.

This time, she would count to ten before looking away, but by the time Morgan counted to five, she had seen the light without a doubt. In fact, there were a series of light flashes...coming in a pattern, a familiar pattern...Could it be?

Dot, Dot, Dot, Dash, Dash, Dash, Dot, Dot, Dot. Morgan realized she was shouting the signals out loud, while jumping up and down. But her reverie was short lived as her tree grove was flooded by Dr. Everett's approaching headlights.

Could Dr. Everett have seen Morgan in the tree grove jumping? Would he find Dakota signaling with a flashlight? To her relief, the signaling stopped as Dr. Everett exited his car, and he never once glanced over towards the grove.

It had never dawned on Morgan and Joel that Dr. Everett might hide Dakota at Souviens. Morgan needed a plan to get into Souviens. But how? Morgan could attempt convincing the police to visit the building... But if they came up empty handed, would that prompt Dr. Everett to take drastic measures to get rid of Dakota? If Morgan ever needed the power of magical thinking that had been demonstrated in their youth, she surely needed it tonight.

THIRTY-EIGHT

Lansing, Michigan
Friday, June 6, 2003
9:05 PM

Philip Pierce watched his mark from behind a large oak tree. It was twilight, and the shadows gave him good cover. The private investigator firm that he had inherited from his old man suited Philip's tastes just fine. He never could have stomached a desk job. The hint of danger kept him from getting board, but the fringe benefits were the best reward.

Philip found it ironic that his father, Samuel, had padded the company coffers with money from Fenton Anderson. Now Philip was growing the company with money from the Misses. Philip had a smattering of other clients, just to make things look legit. But by far, his golden goose was Candace, and her insatiable thirst for information on her husband.

Philip lifted his binoculars and tried to see what Fenton was doing. Fenton came to this cemetery every December eleventh, without fail, but this was the first time Philip had found Fenton visiting in June. So far, the surveillance had been pretty boring, and Philip's mind began to wonder.

He thought back to his inaugural assignment after graduating from college. He had never had one as exciting as that since. His father had told him of a young woman who was proposing a liaison that could be mutually beneficial. Now that Grace had been found, his father Sam's assignments would be drying up. Sam needed to find a new client with deep pockets. Candace proposed that if Sam helped her become Mrs. Fenton Anderson, she would continue to employ his services.

When Philip received the details of the assignment, it sounded like a plot from a Hollywood movie. Candace wanted help in trapping his rich uncle into a marriage. Philip resented his uncle, who had parlayed the inheritance from Sanford Anderson into a successful auto supply company. Philip felt his mother had been short changed in the inheritance distribution. So Philip eagerly volunteered for the duty.

Philip had flown to Las Vegas to help with the scam. His father had connections in Vegas who were more than willing to help with a forged marriage license. Philip had picked up the gaudiest diamond ring he could find at a pawn shop. He helped Candace get his drugged uncle into the bridal suite... And the rest was history.

Still, the best part of the deal had been the fringe benefits. Fenton did not deserve Candace, but Philip fully appreciated her. Not only was she his sexual goddess, she was the most driven woman he had ever met. She had no use for small talk, romance, or other frivolous pursuits. She was goal oriented, and would do whatever it took to reach them.

Philip's reminiscing was interrupted when his mark was starting to move again. Fenton bent down to place something on the ground, and then returned to his car. Once the car was out of sight, Philip left his hiding place to snoop around. A rock was holding down some papers at the grave site for the unidentified victims of the Hotel Kerns fire. Philip picked up the papers and saw that they were a program and a ticket for a medical school graduation ceremony. He stuck the cache in his pocket. One never knew when evidence could come in handy.

Without a doubt, Philip thought, Fenton was a nut. Fenton pursued a woman for years who wanted nothing to do with him. Finally, he gets this unbelievable wife. But instead of enjoying Candace's feminine wiles, Fenton spends his time at this gloomy graveside. Yes, certifiably, a nut.

THIRTY-NINE

Ann Arbor, Michigan
Monday, February 21, 2011
11:15 PM

Officer Brennan had only graduated from the Police Academy several months ago, but he already had quite a collection of unusual stories. This call promised to be bizarre as well. A 911 call had come in from a woman claiming her missing cousin was signaling for help with Morse code from the Souviens Building. Moreover, the woman claimed that the Lansing Police were already familiar with the case. When Officer Brennan had phoned the Lansing precinct, he had been told that the missing woman was a doctor who had survived a kidnapping attempt two weeks ago by a wealthy heiress, only to go missing again the next day.

Well, it sure beat dealing with complaints of rowdy students or traffic accidents, he thought, as he pulled into the Souviens parking lot. He scanned the parking lot for signs of the caller, and saw a figure emerge from a grove of trees behind the building. He was not expecting a six foot tall beauty with a long blond pony tail.

The woman walked up to the officer, and extended her hand, saying, "Thank you so much, Officer, for agreeing to come investigate. I'm positive that Dr. Theo Everett is holding my cousin Dr. Dakota Graham against her will as some type of a lab guinea pig."

Office Brennan listened politely to Morgan's story, bringing him up to date on her theory. Finally, he replied, "Dr. Graham is not officially a missing person at this point. She told her office that she was going on a leave of absence for two weeks. We can't search Souviens as we have no search warrant, and some flashing lights don't constitute an imminent threat to life... But we can go see if this Dr. Everett will agree to voluntarily talk to us."

Morgan appeared somewhat reluctant with this plan, apparently hoping for a more forceful approach. But she agreed to his suggestion, and the duo walked across the parking lot towards the main entrance. They rang the night buzzer, and were answered by a male voice over an intercom. Officer Brennan explained that they were hoping to talk to Dr. Everett about an important issue tonight. The voice, identifying himself as the security guard, stated he would need to check first with Dr. Everett.

Ten minutes later, they were still waiting in the cold weather. Office Brennan was about to ring the buzzer again when the voice returned over the intercom, "Um, Dr. Everett says he can come down to talk with you folks for a few minutes only. He's a really busy guy...But you'll need a security clearance first. Tell me your badge number so I can verify your ID with your post."

There was another ten minute delay before the pair finally found themselves inside the empty lobby of Souviens. The security guard carefully logged in their arrival time, and recorded their demographic information.

"You seem to run a tight ship here, Mr. McCloud," noting the name on his ID badge. "You probably know the name of everyone here in the building at all times." Office Brennan wondered if the guard was a retired cop, who might play along.

However, the guard was not in a talkative mood, and advised them to have a seat in the lobby until Dr. Everett arrived. "I'm worried this is a stalling tactic," whispered Morgan, noting forty minutes had now elapsed since their arrival.

Officer Brennan was about to admit the same thought, when he noted a man in a white lab coat exiting the elevator. The man looked gaunt, haggard, and unshaven, not his idea of a top notch scientist.

Dr. Everett took command of the situation before anyone else could speak. "This is highly irregular, Morgan, insisting on an appointment so late in the evening. But as a courtesy to your cousin, I will give you five minutes of my time."

"When was the last time you've talked to Dr. Graham," asked Officer Brennan, in a tone meant to shift the balance of power in the conversation.

"I drove her home from the hospital as her family members were all off playing on the beach."

Morgan ignored the stab of guilt, and fired back, "Her neighbor saw you putting a clearly intoxicated Dakota in your car, and then driving away. She hasn't been seen since."

A barely discernable pause was noted by both of the accusers before Dr. Everett answered, "She was weak and wobbly from her ordeal, and hadn't eaten in almost a day...I fed her lunch before returning to Ann Arbor...alone."

"Dr. Everett, would you allow us to take a look around your office and lab area?" asked Officer Brennan.

"I don't have time for these games. I am in the middle of ground breaking research. Dr. Graham took a leave of absence from her practice...and from her research here...to recover from the kidnapping attempt. It appears, Morgan, that you and your cousin are no longer confidants. But that's none of my concern. I've already wasted too much time with this silliness. The security guard will see you out and –"

"Of course, I can always awaken a judge for an emergency search warrant if I feel there is imminent danger. The guys sometimes make quite a mess when searching through paperwork and belongings...not to mention the damage to one's reputation...Come on, Morgan—"

Now Dr. Everett interrupted, "I won't stand for my lab being compromised! I'm in the final stages of research, the culmination of my career! Any increase in noise or activity levels in the lab could increase the adrenalin and cortisol levels in the mice. That could drastically alter my testing results."

Dr. Everett's right eye lid was twitching, and he looked close to the breaking point. Officer Brennan almost felt sorry for the frazzled man, but his gut told him that Dr. Everett was hiding something.

"I'm not interested in disturbing your mice or your research, Dr. Everett. I just want to assure that Dr. Graham is not in the premises against her will."

Dr. Everett stood silent for a minute, seeming to weigh the options. "You'll get out of my hair if I give you a tour of my lab?" he asked.

"Lead the way, Dr. Everett," said Officer Brennan.

The trio walked to a bank of elevators and Dr. Everett swiped his ID badge to open the door. They rode to the fourth floor in silence, and then followed Dr. Everett down the hallway to his laboratory. With another badge swipe, they entered his front office. Nothing seemed out of the ordinary to Officer Brennan.

The tour continued into his inner sanctuary, where Dr. Everett played mad scientist, thought Morgan. Her heart was beating through her chest, but she maintained an outwardly calm appearance. She could see no sign of Dakota or of places where someone could be hid. The lab was certainly creepy, with the rows of caged white mice, but otherwise, nothing sinister was evident.

Dr. Everett broke the silence, "Now, I've kept my end of the bargain. Stop wasting my time, and get the hell out of my lab, or I'll call your supervisor in the morning to lodge a formal complaint about police harassment!"

"Thank you for your time, Dr. Everett," said Officer Brennan, as he motioned for Morgan to follow.

Morgan was panicking now, with her worse fear coming true. Dr. Everett now knew she was on to him, and he would need to get rid of Dakota. Focus, she yelled in her brain. There's got to be something she was missing. Officer Brennan walked over to Morgan and gently placed his hand on her back to lead her out of the laboratory area and into the outer office. She kept looking over her shoulder for one last look, one last inspiration.

"I'll need to walk you down to the security desk, company policy," said Dr. Everett, as he picked up his badge and held open the hallway door for the others to follow.

"Wait!" yelled Morgan.

"Morgan, Dr. Everett has shown us his lab. We need to leave now, "said Officer Brennan.

"Listen, I've figured it out! I know what we're missing—" "I must insist you leave —"

Morgan ignored Dr. Everett, and continued talking, "Look, this room has no window. Yet, from the outside, there is a narrow window that runs along the entire length of each floor. I noticed an outside window running along the laboratory area. Could there be a space behind this back wall—"

"I've lost my patience! You both either leave now or I'll—"

"I see what you mean, Morgan...This room doesn't appear as deep as the laboratory area either. "

Officer Brennan and Morgan were ignoring Dr. Everett as they walked back through the open lab door and toward the outer building wall. "The window here in the lab ends at this inner wall, and it is not seen again on the other side in the business office." Officer Brennan studied the row of book cases up against the inner wall. Could these be covering a doorway, he thought.

"Dr. Everett, is there a space behind the outer wall of the business office?" asked Officer Brennan. Officer Brennan turned to face Dr. Everett who had followed the interlopers into the laboratory. In the moment it took to see the Taser in Dr. Everett's hand and then two electrodes with attached wires traveling towards him, Officer Brennan had just enough time to realize he had violated a cardinal rule: Never turn your back on a suspect, no matter how inept he appeared to be.

FORTY

The medical assistant finished taking his vital signs, and then said, "Have a seat, sir. Dr. Graham will be in shortly." The woman exited the room, leaving a Mr. F. Anderson sitting in a guest chair, worrying that he was breaking a promise to Grace.

Fenton had promised never to interfere in the life of Grace's daughter, Charlotte, as long as he lived. He had watched from a distance as Charlotte raised her little girl Eliza. He had rejoiced when Charlotte had become a grandmother. He had grieved when Charlotte lost her daughter, son-in-law, and grandson in a horrific car accident. His heart had broken on learning of Charlotte's Alzheimer's diagnosis.

Fenton had sat in the back row of Eliza's funeral. He had finagled a seat to Dakota's medical school graduation ceremony. But he had never directly interacted with any of Grace's progeny...until today.

Voices drifted through the thin wall of the adjacent exam room. Fenton could hear two women discussing the merits of immunizations. The mother was expressing her views that vaccines were dangerous and ineffective. The young doctor was cogently, but respectfully, making her case that vaccines protect children's lives.

Fenton smiled, remembering the young Grace who was bound and determined to discover a vaccine that would have saved her mother from dying in the 1918 Spanish Flu Epidemic. While fate had intervened in preventing Grace's dream of medical school, her great granddaughter seemed to have picked up the mantle.

Several minutes later, the exam room door opened, and Fenton's reminiscing was interrupted. Had he not known better, Fenton would have sworn that Grace had walked through the door. The resemblance was uncanny.

"Hello, Mr. Anderson. I'm Dr. Graham, a first year resident," she said, reaching out to shake his hand.

They talked for awhile about his medical history and his need for a refill on his blood pressure medication. Then Fenton said, "I couldn't help but overhear your conversation about vaccines."

"Yes, I'm afraid our residency clinic walls are rather thin," she smiled.

"You remind me of a very good friend who as a child lost her mother in 1918 from the Spanish Flu. She was also very passionate about vaccines."

"Historians estimate up to a hundred million people around the world died in that pandemic," Dakota said. "It was an unusual influenza strain in that healthy adults, such as your friend's mother, were hit harder than the typical years where the very young and the very old fare worse."

"So Dr. Graham, what made you go into medicine?"

Dakota thought of the long hours, and debt she was accruing and sometimes wondered herself. "I like to figure things out. I like to ask questions and search for clues to help people solve their problems."

Dakota excused herself to discuss his case with her preceptor, leaving Fenton alone with his thoughts. Those large denomination bills sitting in his safety deposit box belonged to Trevor's descendents, and would certainly take care of Dakota's student loans. More importantly, the story of Grace and Trevor deserved to be told, and their memories preserved. Yes, he thought, he was honored bound by his promise. But wait...He had only promised not to interfere while alive, never saying anything about after his death. As his conscience latched onto this technicality, Fenton began to hatch a plan on how to pass on the memory of Grace and Trevor to their offspring.

FORTY-ONE

Ann Arbor, Michigan
Tuesday, February 22, 2011
12:35 AM

D arl McCloud popped another antacid, but it did little to squelch the boring pain in his gut. These were supposed to have been the golden years for him and his wife when he had retired two years ago as a plant security guard. The plan had been to sell their home and move up North to their cottage.

He had not expected his lazy son to be fired and move back home again, or his daughter and two grandkids to show up on his door after the low life she married had split. Suddenly, there were four more mouths to feed, and their small home was bursting at the seams. Before he knew it, he needed to work as a security guard again to make ends meet. So when that kook Everett had offered to pay him under the table for a few "favors", it had seemed like a no brainer.

At first, Everett only wanted Darl to bend the rules a little. So what if Everett used the MRI on weekends when others were not around...or if Darl forgot to log in the visits of that hottie doctor with the name of a state.

But Darl feared the rules had been bent too far a couple of week ago. Everett had told Darl to disable the security cameras, and to leave his post unattended for a period of time on a Sunday afternoon. Ever since, Everett had been practically living in his lab, bringing food in at all hours of the night.

Darl had been told to notify Everett immediately if anyone showed up sniffing around, asking questions. So when the cop and the blond Amazon woman showed up, Darl had dutifully phoned

Everett. Everett had directed Darl to stall the meddlers for as long as possible before letting them in. Was this Everett character involved in something shady up on the fourth floor that could get Darl into trouble as well?

Darl's stewing was interrupted by the phone ringing. He answered it to hear Everett yelling frantically. "Darl, stop the tall blonde woman who is running down the stairwell towards the lobby. She's vandalized the lab and tased the policeman...I think she may be one of those animal rights nuts...Detain her by any means possible... Don't call the police until I can secure the lab or else all my research will have been in vain! Do whatever it takes to stop her!"

Darl hung up the phone, and stood up from his desk while drawing his firearm. Before he could reach the stair well, the door flew open, with the blonde woman running straight towards him. "Stop right there!" Darl shouted, with his Glock trained on Morgan.

Morgan stopped dead in her tracks, and slowly raised her arms over her head. Then she said very slowly and deliberately, "Dr. Everett has just disabled Officer Brennan with a Taser. As I see it... you have two choices at this point...Let me dial 911, and you can be the hero who saves my cousin from that madman Everett...Or shoot an unarmed woman and have to explain why you did nothing to help a wounded officer upstairs...Now...I'm going to walk across the lobby to make that 911 call. "

Morgan kept her arms elevated as she slowly began walking over to the security desk, never looking back to see that Darl had lowered his weapon. Morgan picked up the receiver, dialed 911, and then yelled the words that she knew would bring the quickest response, "Officer down on the fourth floor of the Souviens Building!"

D r. Everett continued with the steps of his Doomsday scenario that he had been rehearsing in his head since bringing Dakota to Souviens. While that bitch Morgan and the cop had waited in the lobby, he had already started an IV access site in Dakota's arm and sedated her with a barbiturate.

He now gathered his meticulous notebooks from years of research with mice, as well as from his recent discoveries with Dakota. He proudly displayed the culmination of his life's work across his desk top. These journals would seal his legacy as a pioneer in ancestral memory research, and once and for all quiet all the critics that had scoffed and laughed at him.

He also placed a previously type letter on his desk that clearly outlined his theory of ancestral memory, and the ultimate sacrifice he and Dakota would make for the sake of the scientific community. He had finished the letter by stating that he would contact officials with the eventual location of their bodies. The final touch to the letter was attaching Dakota's driver license, which verified her wish for her body to be donated to science.

He needed to move quickly as that wimp Darl was no match for the dominating Morgan. He walked over to Dakota's room, stepping over the still unconscious officer on the floor. He had purchased the Taser thinking he might need to stop a fleeing Dakota, but had never dreamed he would have used the Taser against a policeman. He certainly had not expected the cop to strike his head on the lab bench while collapsing to the ground. Well, he thought, if his Doomsday scenario worked, he would not be around to face the music. He only wished he would be around to hear the accolades for his research.

Dr. Everett rolled the unconscious Dakota onto a sheet, and bent over to pick her up. Although she only weighed 110 pounds, it was all dead weight. The lifting attempt caused Dr. Everett's back to spasm, and he realized how out of shape he had become. A moment of panic set in, but then he eyed the desk chair in the adjoining lab area. He retrieved the chair with caster wheels, and pulled the sheet to slide Dakota onto the chair. Soon he was pushing Dakota down the hallway towards the freight elevator, complete with his bag of drugs in tow.

He loaded his cargo onto the freight elevator and pushed the button for the loading dock. He knew once he exited the building, the security alarm would sound, alerting the others to his departure. Never had every second counted as much as it did tonight.

After giving the details to the 911 operator, Morgan and Darl ran up three flights of stairs, and down the corridor towards Dr. Everett's lab. Darl drew his Glock, and told Morgan to stay behind him as they entered the open business office door and then the open laboratory door. The only apparent activities were the mice moving about their cages.

Morgan found Officer Brennan lying on the floor. He had a steady pulse and was breathing well, but he was still out cold from his head injury. She looked up towards the adjoining wall with the business office and saw that the book cases had been moved out. Just as suspected, there was indeed a doorway to a concealed room.

Darl had already begun investigating. "Somebody's been living here, that's for sure," commented Darl, looking at the rumpled bed, the snack wrappers, and a bath towel hanging on the wall hook.

Morgan ran after him into the secret room, and her heart sunk as she realized the room was empty. "That's Dakota's bed comforter... She was right under our nose, and we let her slip away."

They returned to the lab area, wondering what to do next, when Morgan noticed the elaborate pile of notebooks displayed on Dr. Everett's desk. She walked over and began reading a typed note that appeared to be the crown jewel of the assemblage.

"Oh my God! Everett appears to be planning a murder/suicide event. This mess is all my fault. I stormed the castle without the necessary troops. What do I do now, Darl?" Morgan was normally confident, but tears stung in her eyes in total frustration.

A deafening shrill noise blasted their ears and snapped Morgan back from her paralysis. Darl grabbed her arm and commanded, "That's the alarm from the loading dock exit. Everett just made a run for it. Let's go!"

———∝∝∝———

J oel had worried that Dr Everett would have an elaborate security system at home, but the lock had been surprisingly easy to pick, and entry occurred without a hitch. He had brought latex gloves to avoid finger prints, and a flashlight to avoid drawing attention. But at this point, he actually would have welcome police involvement.

On a daily basis, Joel handled multimillion dollar contracts and investments with confidence and ease. Those wheeling and dealings, however, paled in comparison to this current situation, and he felt way out of his league. He had no idea how to track down a psychopath. He had no idea how to save the only woman he had ever truly loved.

Joel spent the next hour rummaging through drawers and closets, but came up empty handed. The small ranch home had the bare essentials, with no decorating or personal touches added. Dr. Everett apparently kept all his research files at work, as no reference to Souviens or Dakota were found. Joel was flipping through some receipts on the kitchen counter when his cell phone rang.

"Morgan, what's going on at Souviens?"

"Thank God I've reached you. Dr. Everett was keeping Dakota locked up at Souviens as some kind of lab Guinea pig. But he got away from us, taking Dakota with him. He now has offered her dissected brain for the benefit of the scientific community. We've got to find them--fast!"

Joel stood frozen in disbelief, the horror too unimaginable to comprehend.

"Joel? Do you understand me?" asked Morgan.

"Have the police put out an APB on Everett yet?"

"Yes, but that's not going to get results fast enough...Have you found anything at his home to provide a clue where he might take her?"

"This house is so generic that anyone could be the home owner...I was just looking at some recent receipts when you called...Wait...Hold on a minute..."

"Anything?" Morgan pleaded.

"Here's a receipt for a chest freezer, purchased a week ago... Everett's cupboards are bare...He's certainly no chef...Why would he be purchasing a freezer?"

As soon as Joel asked the question, both of them knew the answer. "Does it show where the freezer was delivered?" asked Morgan. "No, but you can bet I plan on waking up every manager of that appliance store tonight until I find out," promised Joel.

"And how do you plan to accomplish that feat?"

Joel thought it ironic that lessons he had learned from his mother might help save Dakota. "Money can make mountains move, and for the first time in my life, I plan on doing just that."

<hr />

D r. Everett pulled into the parking lot of King and Queen Storage, or as he called it, an upscale dumping ground for the consumer indulgences of wealthy Americans. No concrete slab floors or sheet metal walls for this storage site. The storage units here were climate controlled, with drawers and shelves to house the important garbage people charged on their credit cards, and then had no place to store in their Mc Mansions.

But King and Queen offered a feature needed by Dr. Everett: electricity in the storage units. Last week, he had a chest freezer delivered in case his Doomsday scenario occurred. Now he found himself dragging Dakota's limp body from his car to inside his storage unit.

Once the door to the unit was closed, Dr. Everett tried to regain his composure that had been lost since Morgan's unexpected visit. He was having trouble thinking clearly, thanks to sleep deprivation, hunger, and fear.

This was definitely not how he envisioned the last chapter of his research with Dakota. He actually had developed a fondness for the woman, partly due to their common experiences with ancestral memories. Moreover, Dakota was the first professional colleague that had treated him with respect, and had seemed genuinely interested in his theories.

But it was also Dakota's fault that she was in this predicament. Had she followed directions, had she been more precautious, the Doomsday scenario would not have been necessary.

He left the sleeping Dakota on the floor and walked over to examine the freezer, positioned in the middle of the storage unit. He knew that to stop the human decomposition process, Dakota would need to be frozen. He wanted as little damage to the brain tissue as possible before the testing occurred. So his plan was to immediately place her in the chest freezer once he gave her a lethal dose of the barbiturate. He opened the chest, and a blast of frigid air slapped his face.

As he stared into the darkened box, images flashed before his eyes of the dark hole in the ice that had swallowed him alive all those years ago.

He started to shiver uncontrollably. He really did not want to kill her beautiful mind, the perfect embodiment of his theory. But what other choice did he have at this point? Thanks to Morgan's meddling, there were no other options left.

He reflected back on his genealogy discovery that had been the inspiration for all his work. His eleventh great grandfather had been a brave man, who had stood up to the establishment in England, and been hanged for his beliefs. Dr. Everett felt weak compared to his hero. Dr. Everett no longer knew what was right and wrong. He no longer had confidence in his decisions. A year ago, he had dreamed of a Nobel Prize for scientific discovery. Now, he was contemplating murder.

Dr. Everett had hoped that once their research was concluded, Dakota would have been so grateful for answers that she would have overlooked his transgressions. But when Morgan had become involved, he knew all of his hard work would have been halted, and he would have been prosecuted. So he had pulled the trigger on his Doomsday scenario, where at least the research could continue on her brain, and future generations would laud them for their sacrifice and courage...Dying for something that they believed in...just like his ancestor had done so many generations ago.

Dr. Everett no longer had the vivid dreams of the gallows, but he could still sense that great grandfather's strengths. Over the years, when he felt alone and misunderstood, this memory deep inside had sustained him. He closed his eyes for a long while, seeking answers from the very depths of his being.

Eventually, Dr. Everett opened his eyes. He now knew what he needed to do. Yes, there was no joy in this ending, but he knew with certainty what steps were required. Dakota still had her IV site capped off on her arm for easy access to administer drugs. He gathered his bag of supplies and knelt down next to her. But before he started the process, he pulled out his smart phone, and composed a brief email, describing the location of Dakota's body. He sent a timed delivery for three hours from now to Morgan and the authorities. Then Dr. Everett began his work.

∞

I t had been a remarkably easy task after all. First, Joel had contacted a local politician who had business connections in the area. The politician was able to get the home number of the appliance store owner, a campaign contributor. The owner had then called the night janitor who had checked the computer files for the location of the freezer delivery. Now, a little over two hours later, Joel was breaking every speed limit to get to King and Queen Storage.

Joel had notified authorities and Morgan of his discovery, but he was not waiting for their arrival. He knew every second counted tonight, barely slowing down to turn into the empty parking lot. The screeching of his tires was the only noise in the still night air. He stopped his truck a few units away from his destination, grabbed his rifle from behind his truck seat and jumped out. Without thinking of strategy or his own safety, Joel ran to the unit's door, expecting to find it locked. Instead, the door was ajar, with faint light curling around the edges.

Joel slowly opened the door, his rifle cocked and ready. His eyes were drawn to a shiny silver freezer chest in the middle of the unit. He rushed over to the freezer, never praying so hard that he was not too late, and threw open the lid.

But all he found was a blast of frigid air. Tears stung in his eyes, thinking there was still hope. As he turned to leave, Joel spotted something tucked up against the wall. It was a sleeping Dakota, stretched out on a sheet, with a man's coat spread over her for a blanket. And wrapped around her arm was an elastic bandage, where her IV site had once been.

FORTY-TWO

Fenton's thin frame ached from fits of coughing over the last week. His cold symptoms seemed to have settled deeper into his chest. He promised himself he would see a doctor tomorrow; but for now, he just wanted to rest.

Propping himself up with bed pillows, Fenton closed his eyes and realized for the first time that he truly felt his ninety-five years. Whereas most men by now had long since retired, Fenton still went to the office regularly and was involved in important aspects of the company. Despite his rocky start at college, Fenton knew he had made his father proud with his successes at Anderson Technologies. Fenton had been a shrewd business man, but he had always been an ethical and fair competitor.

His personal life was more of a mixed bag. He had endured his long suffering marriage to Candace by escaping on periodic business trips. While she had been a model corporate wife, at home her heart was cold as stone. Having Joel as a son, however, had made his marital misery all worthwhile. A man could not ask for a finer son than Joel.

Still, he wondered had he not had that drink with Candace, could he have returned to Grace's home and talked her into coming back to Lansing. At the very least, he might have been able to call for help when she had the insulin over dosage. Sometimes it seemed like his life was one big series of "what ifs." What if he had not seen Trevor leaving Grace's home so late at night...What if he had controlled his jealousy better...What if he had been honest about Trevor dying in the fire...

His brow felt damp, and he suspected that he was running a fever. He thought about calling Joel for a ride to the emergency room, but decided against bothering him so late at night. Tomorrow would be soon enough.

With a shaking hand, he took a few sips of water from a glass on the night stand. He felt some comfort knowing that his will had been finalized to his wishes. Trevor's money and designs would finally belong to his descendants whom he never knew. But more importantly, with a little perseverance from Dakota to figure things out, Fenton hoped the descendants would come to know about Trevor and Grace.

On his trip to Savannah, Grace had confided in Fenton how Charlotte had come to be. Grace and Trevor were only intimate once, the night before Trevor perished in the fire. No wonder Trevor had been so anxious to get home from the road trip to Jackson and to propose to Grace. Even with the hardships that followed, Grace had been thankful that Trevor would live on through Charlotte.

There was a new "what if" percolating in Fenton's mind. His lawyer Arnold Russell had done his best to dissuade Fenton from making a video will. But Fenton had an ulterior motive. What if Joel and Dakota were to meet? Two wonderfully warm, intelligent, slightly nerdy, and available singles...Who knows where it might lead? There would be a certain poetic justice if Joel and Dakota could find love and happiness together.

Despite his increasing labored breathing, a smile was forming on Fenton's face. He finally felt at peace. He closed his eyes, and drifted off to sleep for the very last time.

FORTY-THREE

S he smelled his aftershave before opening her eyes. Smiling, Dakota
said, "I was hoping you'd be by today."

Joel walked tentatively over to her hospital bed. "Are you up for
some company?"

A still groggy Dakota held out her hand to Joel, and said, "Would
you sit next to me on the bed?"

Joel sat down, still holding her hand. "...You know, it wasn't you that
I didn't trust...It was my old self doubts and insecurity coming to the
surface...I was on my way over to your condo to beg your forgiveness
when my mother beat me to it..."

Dakota raised his hand to gently kiss, then said, "Actually, your
mother told me about your plans before we went on our wild ride...And
Morgan told me about your adventures over the last couple of weeks...By
the way, Morgan has become quite a fan of yours...No easy task to meet
her standards."

They both laughed, and the tension in the room began to dissipate.

Then Joel became silent, and a serious look came over his face. He
looked Dakota in the eyes, and said, "Would it ever be possible for you
to love a man whose mother tried to kill you and succeeded in killing

your great grandmother...And whose father may also have been involved in some type of misdeeds against members of your family?"

Dakota took her free hand and stroked Joel's cheek. The pain in his eyes broke her heart.

"Joel, you're not your parents. Our parents' DNA gives us tools to work with, but it's up to us how we use those tools...I've had a lot of time to think the past couple of weeks. Your parents' and my great grand parents' lives were indelibly intertwined. They all had terrible suffering in their lives...Yes, some of the pain was due to poor decisions on their part...But I see our relationship as a chance to play out their genetic destinies to a different ending, hopefully a happier ending..."

Joel leaned over and kissed Dakota, feeling at home in her arms.

A nurse interrupted them to check Dakota's vital signs, to remove her IV line, and to tell Dakota the doctor would be by to discharge her soon.

After the nurse left, Dakota said, "But there's something I need to talk with you about."

Joel's face clouded over, and said, "Oh oh, nothing good ever starts with the word 'but'..."

He returned to the edge of her bed and tried to fake a smile.

Dakota cleared her throat and attempted to strengthen her resolve. "These past months have brought some incredible gifts to my life, most of all loving you...They've also left me confused about who I am...And I've damaged the relationship with my cousin, my rock when my parents died...all because I lost trust in her love...But it's more than recent events that I need to get a handle on...Most of my life, I've struggled to hide a secret, always feeling that there was something not quite right about me..."

Joel squeezed her hand. "I love you just the way you are... hey, a line from one of my favorite Billy Joel songs," he smiled, this time without faking it.

Dakota smiled back. Then she said, "I just need a little time to figure some things out...to reconnect with Morgan and Aunt Charity...to decide what to do with a million dollars...Could we retry our turkey dinner a couple months from now?"

As much as Joel wanted to begin his life with Dakota immediately, he could also understand why she needed some time to regroup. "You know, I still have that cup of hot chocolate waiting for you next to the fireplace...Couldn't bear to move it until you were back in my life again. Of course, the contents could constitute a science experiment by this time," he chuckled.

Dakota snuggled up against Joel, and said softly, "I haven't thanked you yet for saving my life."

Joel looked down at the woman in his arms, and whispered back, "Thank you for saving my life too."

FORTY-FOUR

Lansing, Michigan
Saturday, August 6, 2011
2:40 PM

On a perfect Michigan summer day, a group of people formed a circle around a grave stone at Mount Hope Cemetery. As the minister recited the Twenty-third Psalm, Dakota gazed at the gathering of her loved ones. On Dakota's right was her fiancé Joel, her hand warm in his. Across from Dakota was Morgan, with her family, and Aunt Charity. Next to Morgan were Tony Davis and his wife, who were enjoying being guests at Aunt Charity's home. And flanking Joel was Dr. Cho, who continued to help Dakota sort out her memory issues.

But the most poignant member of the group was holding Dakota's left hand. Grandma Charlotte seemed to be enjoying her day trip, basking in the August sunshine. For the first time in her life, Charlotte was standing only a few steps away from the father she had never knew, Trevor Moore.

The minister continued to speak, praying not only for the soul of Trevor, but for the other four unidentified victims of the Hotel Kerns fire. After he finished with the Lord's Prayer, all of the assembled were each handed five different colored balloons. Then in unison, the group released the balloons into the cloudless sky.

"What are the balloons for?" asked Charlotte.

"Grandma, We're celebrating the life of Trevor Moore, and four other people, who died in a fire."

"Trevor Moore...I think I remember that name...He was a good man, wasn't he, Dakota?"

Watching the sky fill with a kaleidoscope of colors, Dakota considered if she were more surprised by Charlotte's reported memory of Trevor's name, or by Charlotte remembering Dakota's name for the first time in over a year. Dakota kissed Charlotte's cheek and replied, "He sure was, Grandma."

Later, as Joel and Dakota led the procession of the cars out of the cemetery, Joel mused, "I can't help but wonder how the world might have been different had Trevor lived to produce his bio-waste powered engine...or for that matter, if the electric and natural gas vehicles hadn't been pushed aside by gasoline fueled engine..."

"Trevor's death was a loss on so many levels...My hope is that the scholarship fund will be a legacy to his vision," said Dakota.

Dakota had deduced that the mint condition 1934 currency inherited from Fenton had most likely belonged to her great grandfather, Trevor Moore. While she would never know how Fenton had come to possess these bills, she believed both he and Trevor would have been pleased with their final use to establish the Trevor Moore Scholarship for Alternative Energy Studies.

Dakota leaned back in the truck seat, and closed her eyes. She let her mind drift away with the warm summer breeze coming through the open window. Images from her life flashed across her mind, like still frames of a movie. She marveled at how many of the cherished images included Morgan and Aunt Charity. These common memories bonded them together as a family, as strong as any DNA connection could be.

But her journey over the past months had also allowed her to remember another type of memory. Dr. Everett had never explained how ancestral memories occurred, other than a vague reference to epigenetics. Still, Dakota was confident in their existence. Her memory of the Hotel Kerns fire, as seen through the eyes of her Great Grandmother Grace, had forever forged a new family bond.

"Je me souviens..."

"Pardon?" said Joel.

"French for 'I remember', if my recollection of high school verb conjugations is correct," replied Dakota.

"Also displayed on license plates as the official motto of the Providence of Quebec," said Joel.

"Trivia points for my favorite history buff," Dakota laughed.

"...You know...I haven't brought up your captivity at Souviens because you've been in the middle of processing all that with Dr. Cho...But when or if you ever want to talk about that monster Everett, you know I'm here for you...."

Dakota shivered at the possible fate that had loomed before her. But she was making good progress with Dr. Cho in putting her time as a lab experiment behind her. Just as Dr. Everett had predicted, her memories of the Hotel Kerns fire had become much more muted and hazy. She no longer was at the mercy of her ancestral memories controlling her life. By remembering, she had been set free.

Dakota could not help but wonder why Dr. Everett had let her go. The police still had no leads on his whereabouts, and she doubted he would ever allow himself to be captured. But Dakota had a theory on why Dr. Everett had spared her life. She believed that in the end, he too had remembered his past, and those ancestral memories had set him free.

FORTY-FIVE

Ann Arbor, Michigan
Thursday, April 14, 2039
9:40 AM

Bryce Anderson traveled the sixty-five mile trip from Lansing to Ann Arbor in a little under thirty minutes on the Bullet Train. The station was close to her final destination, so she decided to finish the trip by walking. Besides, the fresh air would help clear her head.

Three years out of graduate school, she had landed her dream job as an investigational reporter for a major television news show. She had produced some respectable pieces, but nothing with pizzazz, nothing that would put her on the map.

Then a couple months ago, she had a brainstorm for covering a current story, but from a unique angle. Getting the approval from her boss had been the easy task. The more daunting task had been getting her parents' approval, as they would be an integral part of the story. But after several family discussions with her parents and siblings, Bryce had finally been given the green light.

So now she was heading towards the Souviens building, where she was to meet her production crew in the parking lot. In the past decade, Souviens had become one of the wealthiest corporations in America, a long way from the small startup company thirty years ago. Their discoveries had revolutionized the field of psychiatry. This in itself would have been an interesting tale. However, Bryce knew the back story, which with its human dimensions, could really help her show's ratings.

As she neared the Souviens building, she spotted her two crew members with their equipment in tow. The trio entered the outside door and was greeted by a hologram receptionist.

"Welcome to Souviens, where yesterday's memories are applied to today's problems. Please procedure to our security station for your retinal scan," said a professional looking woman's projection with a hint of a British accent.

One by one, each member stepped into an anteroom, where they were photographed and identified with a retinal scanner. Then they gathered in the main reception area to wait for their host, Garrett McIntyre, the CEO of Souviens.

While they waited, Bryce reviewed her mental notes in her head. Two decades ago, Souviens had rocked the scientific community with their claim that memories could be passed between generations. Actual experiences of an ancestor could be remembered by her progeny. This was a fascinating idea, but ideas in themselves don't bring revenue to a company. A commercial usage would need to be found for the startup company to thrive.

It was not long after that Souviens proposed a theory regarding patients suffering from anxiety disorders. That feeling of anxiety for no apparent reason might be the remnants of an actual terrifying experience witnessed by an ancestor. Or an inordinate fear of snakes, for example, might be a life's lesson learned from a forbearer. This theory evolved into treatment regimens for medication resistant anxiety disorders; and the subsequent FDA approvals have made the share holders of Souviens extremely wealthy.

One of her co-workers nudged her arm to get her attention. Exiting the elevator banks was the elusive Mr. McIntyre himself. Souviens rarely talked to the press, but with additional FDA approvals pending, the company was making a bit of a publicity push. Mr. McIntyre walked over to their group, and extended his hand.

"It's a pleasure to meet you, Ms. Anderson. I'm a big fan of your show. Let's go over to a conference room for some refreshments and discussion."

Mr. McIntyre reminded Bryce of an actor that would be hired to play a president in a movie. He flashed some perfectly capped teeth as he led the way. She wondered what his reaction would be if he knew that Souviens' first test subject had been her mother, Dakota Graham Anderson.

The group settled around a conference table, complete with their caffeinated beverage of choice. After some small talk, Mr. McIntyre asked, "Unusual name you have, Ms. Anderson. Is there a story behind it?"

"My mother continued a family tradition of naming children based on where they were conceived...I was a honeymoon baby... Bryce Canyon."

"Interesting...Well, let's get down to business. I trust the interview schedule I sent you meets with your approval. So if you'll follow me, we'll start with one of our scientists that can explain the science behind our discoveries and—"

"Excuse me, I don't mean to interrupt, but I was hoping we could briefly interview you as well ...in order to learn a little of the history behind this discovery. Who was the scientist with the 'ah-ha' moment, or the initial inspiration?"

Mr. McIntyre paused for a moment before replying. "These discoveries were more of a collaborative effort. As for your interviewing me for your piece, my expertise is more in finance... I think our scientists will better serve your needs. So, let us proceed."

Bryce followed Mr. McIntyre out of the conference room. Souviens could not claim that Bryce did not give them an opportunity to give Dr. Everett and her mother their due. For reasons Bryce did not fully understand, it was very important to her mother that Dr. Everett be credited with his discoveries. Whether it was some form of Stockholm syndrome, or a compassionate heart, Dakota had forgiven Dr. Everett and felt protective of his accomplishments.

Bryce remembered the first time she had heard Dr. Everett's name mentioned. A policeman named Officer Brennan had come to their home when she was a child to inform her parents that Dr. Everett had been found dead in a low rent hotel room in California. Despite money in his pocket, and food in the room, it appeared Dr. Everett had died of malnutrition six years after kidnapping Dakota. Her mother believed Dr. Everett had simply lost the will to live. Besides the cemetery employees, her parents were the only people at the graveside when Dr. Everett was buried.

Bryce and her crew were lead to another conference room where Mr. McIntyre introduced them to Dr. Sunita Jain, their lead microbiologist. The crew set up their equipment, and Bryce settled in and began her interview.

"Dr. Jain, we appreciate your taking the time to educate our viewers about ancestral memories. In layman's terms, could you summarize how it is possible for the memory of an ancestor to be passed to her descendants?"

"Certainly. But I must state up front, we still have large gaps in our understanding of this phenomenon. Scientists have known for a long time that strong emotions surrounding an event can help reinforce a memory. Souviens made a quantum leap when discovering that under extreme duress, not only are memory signals reinforced in the brain, but neurohumoral signals are sent outside the brain to our other body tissues."

"So memory signals can end up in any of our other organs...even, for example, our liver?" asked Bryce.

"Technically yes, but during the early dividing of the embryo, the cells destined to become our liver have the DNA that pertains to other body functions turned off by epigenetics. So even if there is a memory signal in a liver cell, this signal has nowhere to go."

"What is the destination of these neurohumoral signals then?" asked Bryce.

"It turns out that these signals can reach developing egg cells in a mother's ovaries. If one of these egg cells is successfully fertilized, the resultant embryo will become a pluripotential cell...In other words, a cell capable of creating all cell lines, including the central nervous system."

"And thus, these signals can carry the ancestral memory to the developing embryo's brain?"

"Precisely," answered Dr. Jain.

"But I would hazard a guess that most of my audience has never experienced such a memory."

"There's much more to the story. We need to go back to human origin to understand the importance of ancestral memories. For example, there would be a real evolutionary advantage if a mother

could pass on fear of an advancing bear to her offspring. Buried in what was once referred to as our junk DNA because its purpose was unknown are genes responsible for ancestral memory amplification. These genes code for proteins that continuously renew our ancestral memory."

Dr. Jain paused for a drink of water. Bryce hoped she would not lose her audience with too technical of an explanation. Bryce would need to insert some computer animation on final editing to make the story come alive.

Dr. Jain picked up the story again. "But as mankind evolved, we theorize that these ancestral memories became more of a burden than an advantage. These memories created fear and hesitation, and discouraged exploration of one's world. Furthermore, children stayed with their parents longer, allowing more time to learn from parental teachings and less need for ancestral memories."

"How did mankind overcome these fears and set out to conquer the world?" asked Bryce.

"Over time, some descendants had portions of the genes that control ancestral memory amplification turned off via methylation. These changes gave some humans decreased ability to recall ancestral memories, but an increased evolutionary advantage over their fearful brethren. Eventually, most of mankind no longer had awareness of ancestral memories."

"You use the word 'awareness'. Does this mean most of us still have ancestral memories but they are under the radar, so to speak?" asked Bryce.

"That is correct. However, with enough stress in one's life, these genes may start to turn on again, resulting in a partial awareness. This background memory could trigger anxiety and panic in an individual for no recognized reason"

Bryce decided it was time to swing the discussion over to how Souviens had capitalized on these discoveries. "It's one thing to revolutionize the field of microbiology. It's another thing to spring board from the conceptual to a very practical use in helping people with resistant anxiety disorders. How was this leap accomplished?"

Dr. Jain hesitated, and looked down at her notes. "I guess just the fertile imagination of our workers. This would probably be a good time to segue to your next interview. Dr. Demetri is a psychiatrist with expertise in treating anxiety disorders. I believe Mr. McIntyre is waiting outside to escort you." Dr. Jain abruptly stood up to confirm the interview was over.

Bryce laughed under her breath that employees at Souviens were not good at lying. Dr. Everett and her mother had learned by their own experiences long before any fertile imagination at Souviens occurred that ancestral memories were amplified by extreme emotions and were quieted by learning the historical context of the memories. When Dr. Everett had eluded Morgan and absconded with Dakota, he had left behind volumes of journals, filled with his life's work, prominently displayed. Souviens would subsequently claim these discoveries as their own.

Bryce's crew packed up, and they were led to their next interview with Dr. Ari Demetri. For Bryce, this would be more than an interview. This would be a stepping off point for her own personal journey.

Dr. Demetri was a short, round man with a jolly expression. He reminded Bryce of a Santa Claus without the beard. He enthusiastically shook her hand as the crew got down to business again.

Dr. Demetri settled into his office desk chair, and Bryce began the interview. "Dr. Demetri, Souviens has become one of the richest corporations in America, thanks to its patented treatment protocols for treating medication resistant anxiety disorders. Can you explain to our viewers how these treatments work?"

"I believe Dr. Jain has brought you up to speed on how partially remembered ancestral memories can create anxieties and fear in people. Once these memories are brought to the surface, they can be put to rest with proper education and therapy. The trick was figuring out how to bring them to the surface."

"As I remember, it was quite a struggle to receive your original FDA approval," commented Bryce.

"It was so unlike any previous medical treatments that there was tremendous resistance initially. But our success stories have won over even the skeptics."

"Would you take us through the steps of the treatment protocol?" asked Bryce.

"First and most importantly, we select our patients very carefully. In addition to thorough psychiatric evaluations, patients must undergo full cardiopulmonary testing to assure their safety. Once cleared, a patient must agree to close follow up after the treatment, for that is when the healing process takes place."

Bryce's mind began to wander from the interview. For the first time, she started to feel a little apprehension about her plan. She forced her attention back to Dr. Demetri.

"The key is to cause a surge in stress hormones. Patients receive a proprietary infusion of chemicals that simulate our biochemical response to stress. Cardiac rhythm and brain waves are closely monitored."

"How do patients describe this experience?" asked Bryce.

"A combination of exhilaration and fear, such as you might expect with a first parachute jump."

"When do the ancestral memories resurface?"

"Hours to days after this treatment. Patients are required to reside in treatment centers for two weeks after their treatments. They meet regularly with historians, and psychologists to put their memories into the appropriate historical and emotional context. Once discharged, patients will be closely followed as outpatients over several months."

Bryce decided it was time to turn the interview to Souviens' new FDA applications for a controversial usage of their treatment protocol.

"Dr. Demetri, some say that the soaring profits generated when Souviens' treatment first hit the market have flattened out in recent years. Now, you have a new FDA application pending for other usages of your treatment. Your critics claim that you would be exposing healthy patients to potentially dangerous drugs, all for the sake of expanding your revenues. How do you respond?"

"Our new application is not for medical treatments. We have now expanded our protocol to healthy patients who also want to explore their pasts. By our very nature, humans are explorers. We have conquered the continents, the seas, and outer space. But our minds remain a vast frontier, barely explored. "

"I understand you have a long waiting list for this experience if the FDA approves your request," said Bryce.

"That is correct, Ms. Anderson. We are currently undergoing clinical trials, and I understand you have been approved to be a test subject."

Bryce had always been the adventurous one in the family. She had been saving for years to afford a ticket to the moon settlement. She was definitely no shrinking violet. So when her producer had suggested Bryce becoming part of the story, she had jumped at the chance.

Bryce had enlisted the help of her parents to provide background interviews on the real story behind Souviens success. However, Bryce had failed to mention her plan to participate in the clinical trials. Bryce adored her parents, and was very close to them. But her patents worried so much about her that she decided to spare them the additional stress. Now she had to admit that she was having some butterflies about her decision.

Dr. Demetri was continuing to talk about the virtues of their new drug protocol. "Our test subjects so far have found the experience to be a fascinating trip through their ancestry, with no greater problems than our placebo groups. If you are ready, Ms. Anderson, I will take you to the nurse that will get you ready for a journey of many lifetimes."

Her crew that would be recording her journey tagged along as Dr. Demetri led her to the fourth floor of the Souviens building. She wondered how close she would be to the room where her mother had been held captive.

Dr. Demetri introduced Bryce to Sarah, the nurse who would be prepping Bryce for the treatment. Sarah asked Bryce to provide her medical records, which included her cardiopulmonary and psychiatric clearances. Bryce passed her forearm under a scanner that retrieved her medical information stored in an implanted chip.

"I'm going to leave you in Sarah's capable hands. Bon voyage, Bryce. I will be anxious to learn the stories of your journey." With that sendoff, Dr. Demetri bid her farewell.

Sarah directed Bryce to a changing room. Once outside the prying eyes of the cameras, Bryce put on the cotton hospital gown and tied it in the front, as she had been directed. Bryce looked at her image in the mirror. She laughed that no one could accuse her of obsessing over her image. Hospital gowns were never flattering to anyone. "It seems like after all these years, someone would have designed a better gown," she muttered under her breath.

She remembered the new advertising mantra of Souviens, "Memory: the final frontier". It was a takeoff on the opening line from the television show Star Trek that had been popular over seventy years ago. Her nervousness was becoming replaced by anticipation as she imagined what she might discover. What had her ancestors faced? What conflicts had they overcome? As she stepped out of the dressing room, she was more determined than ever to find out.

FACT VERSUS FICTION

This book is a work of fiction. All speaking characters are not real. To my knowledge, there is no company named Souviens, and no scientific basis for ancestral memories.

However, part of the inspiration for this novel came from a very real tragedy. In 1934, the Hotel Kerns located in Lansing, Michigan, burned to the ground, killing thirty-four people, including seven Michigan legislators. I was haunted by the story of the five unidentified victims. What were their backgrounds? Why were they traveling through Lansing? What did their families think when they never returned home?

This novel provides a fictionalized account of one of the unidentified victims. With that exception, the facts and the descriptions of the hotel tragedy, based on my historical readings, reflect the actual events to the best of my knowledge.

The characters were frequently placed in many authentic settings. Actual landmarks, businesses, cultural events, and collegiate facts were incorporated into the novel to help illustrate the rich tapestry of Mid-Michigan life.

The scientists in the novel make references to epigenetics. This is not fiction, but rather a rapidly growing scientific field, demonstrating that experiences of parents can alter the genetic expression of their progeny.

Many of us feel a kinship with the people who have come before us. This interest fuels the passion of many genealogists. Could there be some kernel of truth that deep in our psyche we do have some remembrance of our ancestors? While there is no scientific proof to support this hypothesis, it is fun to wonder, nonetheless. I hope you enjoyed the novel.

ABOUT THE AUTHOR

Barbara Saxena is a family practice physician in Grand Ledge, Michigan. She is a graduate of General Motors Institute, University of Michigan, and Michigan State University College of Human Medicine. In her free time, she can be found walking her pack of golden retrievers.